TROPICON ISLANDS

TROPICON ISLANDS

ISLANDS

LEXXICON

PROLOGUE

ADONIS THOMAS FELT lightheaded.

The backstage area smelled of weed. Extraordinarily strong weed.

"Secondary smoke is a thing," he said to himself because he was not a smoker. He was walking down a narrow corridor towards the changing rooms. In his hands were two cans of soda and a packet of fish and chips. He could hear the muffled boom of loud music coming from the stage, and the cheers of the crowd. The beauty of being backstage was you could separate yourself from the crowd's direct energy yet still get a sense of it and prepare your mind to face it. He wasn't alone in the corridor. There were security bouncers every few meters to keep away any groupies or strange characters. He nodded a greeting as he passed each one of them, eventually getting to the door he was aiming for. The smell of weed was strongest here. Taking a deep breath before he went in wasn't going to help.

He opened the door and went in. Predictably, it was slightly stuffy inside, eased only by the air conditioning that was running. Soft hip hop music was playing from a portable radio. It was a sparsely furnished room with a leather couch along one wall and a small coffee table in front of it. The only other seat faced a dressing room mirror. Seated on it was the young singer-rapper Oceania. In her hands was a guitar, which she was strumming along to the radio music. Behind her was a makeup artist combing up the rapper's hair, the largest natural afro he had ever seen on a woman. The comb was going through it so slowly and gently it looked therapeutic.

His arrival made Oceania look up at his reflection in the mirror. He stood at an angle where he could see her and his reflection too, although the room's dim lighting meant he wasn't too visible. His short hair was a little frazzled, and his goatee had grown a few inches longer. He was never keen on keeping a trim when on the road. He was beginning to lose his athletic frame as he couldn't run in the mornings anymore.

"You got it?" Oceania asked, in her husky voice. Her speaking voice was always toned down, giving her this gruff vibe. Her rapping voice was higher pitched. He always marveled at her ability to switch between the two.

"Sure," he replied, advancing towards her with the package. He placed it atop the dressing table beside bottles of hair products, combs, and makeup.

"Thank you, darling. Have I told you that you're one of the best?"

"You always say that."

She laughed at this, her laughter a little more drawn out

than usual. As she calmed down, she lifted her right hand to take a short puff of the weed she was smoking.

"Wanna take a drag?" she offered.

"Nah, I'm good," he replied.

"Your loss," she replied nonchalantly. That was one of the magical things about Oceania. You could throw little things like a rejected offer or bigger things like a beef with a fellow musician and she would walk it off as if nothing happened, like water off a duck's back.

"Are you good?" he asked.

"Yeah, I'm good. Pass me the soda, I'm getting a little parched," she said. He handed her one can and she popped it open and took a sip.

"So, when are we getting paid for this?" she asked before downing a handful of chips.

"We?" he asked, puzzled.

Chewing as she spoke: "Yeah. After I do the show, how long will it be before we are paid?"

"Um, I'm just an intern here. I honestly can't tell you much about that." Adonis didn't know what to make of it.

"But you are a smart intern. That's why the big and wonderful entertainment company brought you here," she said with a smile. "They know you can handle me."

"I'm not sure about that."

The combing was done now, her hair was looking full and vibrant. He was amazed and got even more distracted when she spun in her seat to face him. She wore a long-sleeved body suit with military gear patterns. It had a deep V-neck that give a hint of her bosom. The figure-hugging outfit came short of her knees, revealing smooth and oiled up legs. She was a stunning woman with a street edge.

"I'm sure you can handle all of this and then some," she said, as she playfully bit on a single piece of chips with her eyes on him. He felt blood rush to his cheeks for a moment. She had never teased him like this before.

"You play too much," he managed to say.

Oceania stood up and slowly walked towards him, exaggerating the sway of her hips with each step until she stood right in front of him. The single chip was still on her lips, with one end poking out as she moved her face close to his.

"I would play much more if you let me," she somehow said without dropping the chip, inviting him to bite it.

The make-up artist was wide-eyed, keen to see where this was going.

"I think you should finish up. You are about to hit the stage," Adonis said, as he retreated towards the door.

"I will. Just tell me one thing: why are these guys still holding on to my money? We've done three shows together on the road so far, I have four more shows after this one, and I have no money in my account yet. You think that's cool?" she asked, her tone turning serious.

"I honestly don't know anything about the deal you signed. I'm just here to make you comfortable."

"Well, it doesn't look like you can do that. But I appreciate your honesty."

"Maybe we should wait for Gunner to return, he can tell you more," he said, trying to change the direction of the conversation.

"You think the Hulk will tell me that or break me in half?"

"He can't break you in half, you are one of our top artists. Trust me, he values you," Adonis replied, massaging her ego.

Oceania went quiet for a moment, searching his face.

Then she burst out laughing, holding her ribs as she moved back towards the dressing table. She leaned onto the seat and took another puff of her weed before placing it on an ashtray.

"I think I watched too many gangster movies. Why one earth am I trying to shake down an intern?" Oceania asked, more to herself than to anyone in the room. She shook her head and laughed some more. "I really hope these guys pay me soon, otherwise I may have to get wild in this bitch."

"I don't think that's a very smart thing to do," a deep voice bellowed from behind Adonis.

Oblivious to them, Gunner Brown had popped open the door. Adonis had unwittingly left it ajar. None of them had noticed him, nor knew how much he had heard.

Oceania just shrugged, suddenly unwilling to speak.

Adonis stepped out of the way as Gunner walked in. Oceania had earlier called Gunner the Hulk not because he was Mr. Olympia, but because he was heavily built. Just over five feet tall, he was shorter than expected. Yet, he had an aura of gentility to him, mixed with a hint of violence that was never too far behind. A few scars on his neck and forearm gave you the idea he had fought a few bruising battles and survived.

Gunner loathed it when people talked behind his back. He had spies to do that to other people, but not to him or the company he represented. So, he wasn't planning on letting Oceania off the hook so easily.

"You want to tell me what's troubling you?" Gunner asked, his eyes trained on her.

"I was just saying… um. It would be nice to get a little cash while I'm on tour," Oceania said.

"But we had a deal about this right?"

"Yeah, about that... Man. The deal feels like shit right

now. You know. It's not connecting with my reality right now, you feel me?" Oceania replied, the weed in her veins making her bolder. This was good courage for her to do her shows, but not for conversations with the likes of Gunner.

Gunner, reading the room, addressed the makeup artist. "Her ten minutes are up. You are done?"

"Yes, I'm done," the makeup artist replied.

"Good. Let's go on stage, Oceania." Gunner said, opening the door wide open.

Adonis half-expected Oceania to pull a stunt, but she knew better than to stretch herself too far. She picked up her guitar, and swaying hips and all, sauntered out of the room.

Adonis followed Gunner and Oceania as they headed to the stage area. The corridor got darker the closer they got, but this was numbed by the sound of the cheering fans growing louder and louder. He had been told there were about five thousand people on this show alone, and he wished he could see it for himself. But the power of such charm belonged to the gifted Oceanias of this world and he respected that.

They got to the steps that would lead to the deck, which was going to lift her up to the stage for her dramatic entrance. Gunner stopped her before she climbed up. He leaned forward too. Although he was whispering, Adonis could make out his words to her:

"Now, I know sometimes these things can be difficult to grasp, but I can tell you right now that we have your back. If there's anything you need, let me know. Talk to me, not to the intern or anyone else. Talk to me. By the time you get off that stage, I will have taken care of it."

Oceania nodded.

He continued, "Let me not hear that you've been talking

to other people about this ever again. It makes me angry, and I don't think you want to make me angry. Now, go out there and put on a show!"

Gunner ended his motivational threat with a gentle squeeze on her arm, and Oceania turned away and went up the steps. She wasn't broken down, the spring on her step still evident. Like water off a duck's back.

Adonis watched her as she finally stood on the deck, at the marked center position that would give her perfect balance as she went up. A stagehand checked on her to see if she was fine, then backed away. As the smoke machines came on, the deck started going up. She turned towards them and, looking straight at Adonis, she blew him a kiss followed by a smile. He gushed again as he watched her disappear into the stage above.

Cheers suddenly erupted, and the energy of her star power could be felt by all, even by the two men backstage.

Their gem had arrived.

CHAPTER ONE

So, you say you like wild things
Right now, you got it all wrong
See all my cash take it all in
Only my vibe can make it last long.

THE LYRICS TO the song filtered to Adonis's ears as he pushed the loaded office trolley down the hallway. The music was never loud. The advanced surround sound music system made sure it was just soft enough to catch your attention whenever you walked into the Sephtis Entertainment lobby. It was complemented by a large LED screen mounted on the wall. The screen stretched the expanse of the wall, from floor to ceiling, just falling shy of the horizontal margins of the wall. A music video would play for thirty seconds on average, before shifting back to the Sephtis logo: the silhouette of a musician's skinny form and flowing shock of hair jumping up while holding a microphone aloft. It was a logo full of energy that made you immediately think of music, performance, energy, and reaching for the stars – which is what the company was there to do.

It's one of the things that Adonis loved about the space. But he didn't have the time to think about that much or to watch the music video. He only had five minutes to do the rounds of the whole floor, dropping off letters and parcels at various department desks.

The open plan office was colorful and almost casual. The walls were plain white or subtle gray in most parts, broken by oil pastel paintings that added a charm to the feel of the place, as if you were in an art gallery. Rumor was that the art pieces were from the boss's personal collection, and some were worth millions of dollars. Adonis didn't like rumors or conspiracy theories, so he made a note to image search a few of them and form his own conclusions. It wasn't high on his priority list.

Customized black swivel chairs with high backs dotted the office landscape, their spread broken by warm-colored seats with unconventional shapes that were found across the space. The colored ones were mostly to charm staff and guests into a casual stance. They were also found in the gaming and coffee rooms, as well as the custom mini bar. Basically, the space invited you to work and play in the literal sense.

Adonis dropped off an envelope at Marty's desk.

"Thanks, man."

He was on his way to the next desk when he heard a gruff voice behind him.

"Hey, A.D, come over here." Adonis knew who it was and turned on his heel.

Gunner's head was peeking out of the boss's door. Adonis always wondered why he called him A.D., but he figured it was because Adonis was possibly an unnecessary mouthful for him.

"Yes, boss." Adonis replied.

"Don't call me that. You know my name. Make a cup of coffee for the man you should call boss. Strong, no sugar, okay?" Gunner ordered.

"Sure. Can I—"

"Drop the trolley thing. Make it quick," Gunner said, as he closed the door.

Adonis parked the trolley along the wall and headed for the office kitchen. It was a large kitchen with the latest appliances you needed to fix a meal. Standing out from all of them was a Mocha pot. Adonis had quickly learned that the boss loved his coffee made from it. He got the Ethiopian coffee beans into the grinder as he heated water in the bottom pot on the stove. He then placed the granules in the basket and screwed the top of the pot to the bottom and placed the pot back on the stove on low heat. He watched carefully as the black coffee started filling the top pot. He let it go on for a few minutes and then turned off the stove. As he poured it into a cup, he silently prayed the coffee was not too bitter.

He knocked on the boss's door. Gunner opened it, and Adonis walked in.

The last time he had been there was three months ago, when he was being introduced on his first day of internship. Vernon Wilson was a big man – tall, with wide shoulders and a solid frame. Adonis knew that Vernon was big on working out, and his consistency probably made him look younger for a man in his early fifties.

"Here's your coffee, sir," Adonis said, as went to place the coffee on the polished mahogany desk.

"Thank you, Adonis, bring it to me," Vernon said, motioning the young man to walk over.

Adonis walked quickly but steadily to Vernon, feeling the softest of footfalls courtesy of the rich carpet that covered the whole floor of the office.

Vernon took the steaming cup and took a quick sip. Adonis held his breath as Vernon swirled the coffee in his mouth like a wine taster. He then swallowed it and smiled.

"I think I have found my coffee man," Vernon said to Gunner.

"He's a sharp boy," Gunner answered.

"Is this true?"

Adonis blurted out the first thing that came to mind.

"My momma taught me from a young age."

Vernon nodded slowly as he sipped again, his eyes on the young man.

"You used to do a few gigs before you came here, right?" Vernon asked.

"Yes, I had started a small company with a friend of mine," Adonis replied.

"What kind of company?"

"I shouldn't call it a company really. Just a startup based in my friend's home. We came up with an app that allowed us to curate events on the island," Adonis explained.

"What happened to it?"

"It's still there. We slowed down a bit because of life and stuff."

"You designed it yourselves?" Vernon asked.

"Yes. Just the two of us. Took us eight months."

"I see. So, you love the party scene?" Vernon asked.

"More like the music scene. Of course, that always leads to the party scene, so I guess you could say that. I don't go crazy or anything like that."

"I didn't say you do," Vernon replied. He took the last sip and handed the cup back to Adonis. *That was fast*, Adonis thought.

Vernon walked back to the large window. "Your internship ends in two weeks?"

"Yes, sir," Adonis replied, with a sense of dread.

Vernon nodded slightly. "Thanks for the coffee."

Adonis looked at Gunner, who waved him to get out. The meeting was over. Adonis left, feeling a strange sense of unease. As if something had been taken from him, but he didn't know what it was.

↑

Adonis got home and was glad to get the pleasant whiff of chicken stew. He was exhausted, but his hunger was stronger.

"Is that you, Gail?" his mother's voice beckoned from the kitchen.

"No Ma, it's me."

"Ahh. Hello, my husband." Adonis smiled as he headed to the kitchen. He knew why she called him that and didn't mind it much.

"What's smelling so good?" he asked, teasingly stretching out his hand towards the cooker. Bernice Thomas, his mother, tapped it away.

"You're not thirteen anymore to be trying that with me!" she said. He laughed as he watched her stir the pot with the steaming piecing of chicken bobbing up and down. His stomach rumbled in anticipation.

Bernice was an overweight woman who always wore colorful outfits to match her personality. She was full of life and one of the hardest workers he knew.

"Please tell me it won't be long," he said.

"What's the rush? It's just thirty more minutes."

"Gail is not home?"

Bernice sighed. "She's supposed to be back from that after-school program. She's running late now."

Adonis frowned at this. Gail had recently joined an after-school class. They always stuck to their hours so that their students could get home before dark.

"She's not been late for the past few weeks, so there must be a good reason. Don't worry about it," he reassured her.

As he said this, he was dialing Gail's phone. She didn't answer. He wasn't going to worry.

"Gail is a young girl though. I can't have her getting comfortable with that," Bernice said. She was always strict, raising her kids, now adjusting without their father. She had mellowed in recent years, but she hadn't lost her touch.

"I won't let her," Adonis said.

She grunted. "Leave me to my cooking or I will mess up your food."

Adonis smiled and backed out of the kitchen to wait for his sister.

Gail got back home just before dinner, claiming she was delayed when the bus broke down. Her usual bubbly self was forced to cower down as her mother scolded her because she didn't return calls nor text messages sent to her. Gail apologized and ate her dinner in muted fashion. Adonis knew it was all a show, and that she was just relieved to get home in one piece. Marissa, the last born, was her quiet self, listening in on conversations while digging into her meal. She ate as little as she spoke, yet her frame was not a little one.

"This chicken slaps, Momma. It should be part of the graduation party menu," Gail whispered. She was clearly working to get back into her mother's good books.

"What did you say?" Bernice asked.

Marissa jumped in: "She says your chicken is great. Can we have it when Addie graduates?"

"What party are you talking about here?" Bernice was not playing along.

"Come on, it's going to be the first graduation in the family since well, you. It's not just for Adonis, it's a party for you too. It's the first major milestone since… well … since Terek left," Marissa replied.

Marissa rarely spoke, but she had the uncanny talent of speaking weighty words when she did.

"You don't need to talk about him to convince me," Bernice said. It had been five years since their father Terek had walked out of their lives that rainy July morning. She had never looked back. She wasn't angry anymore. The pride of her efforts was seated at the table with her.

"I'll sleep on it," Bernice said. "Now eat up fast before it gets cold."

↑

"By virtue of the authority vested in me by the board of trustees, I hereby confer upon you the degree for which you have completed all the requirements and expressly…"

Adonis hadn't really listened to the Vice Chancellor because it felt like an out of body experience. As he walked back to his seat, wearing his graduation gown, he lifted up the parchment as his eyes locked on his family members. They were all clapping, his mother fighting back tears. He walked up to her and they embraced, the stress and struggle they shared to get him there very real, and now gone. It was a moment of freedom.

When they loosened their embrace, Bernice was smiling again, as if the embrace had dried all her tears.

"I'm proud of you, my husband," Bernice said to him. He was happy to make her proud – nothing else mattered.

"You made it all possible, Ma. I'll keep making you proud," Adonis replied.

After getting hugs from his sisters, Adonis turned his gaze to Dmitri Morisson. The two best friends embraced with a special palm greeting that they had done since high school.

"You did it, man!" Dmitri said, gushing with pride at his friend's achievement. He had been Adonis's sounding board for many nights when things were not going well – the dark days when his mother struggled with college fees. That's when they started the company, and some of the little pennies they earned helped ease things along. This was a victory Dmitri shared, and he was glad to see Adonis stronger now.

"We did it! Thank you for walking with me, man," Adonis said with deep sincerity. Dmitri was a genius, and he couldn't imagine going forward in his career without him in it.

"To many more victories," Adonis added.

"To many more!" Dmitri replied.

The brotherly banter was interrupted by a chilling shriek that pierced through that sunny day. He turned swiftly to see

his mother Bernice fall to the ground. He thought she was collapsing. It was as he was moving towards her that he realized
Gail was on the ground, convulsing, froth coming from her
mouth, her eyes glazing over. In a panic, Bernice tried to hold
her up. Marissa was frozen in fear. Adonis was by Bernice's
side in a flash, helping her attend to Gail. None of them knew
what to do.

"Call an ambulance!" Adonis shouted at Dmitri.

↑

The hospital walls were cream in color, punctuated by brightly
colored balloons, flowers, and rainbows. In another moment, it
might have lifted the mood, but it wasn't working for Adonis.

The doctors had asked them to leave as they pumped her
stomach, especially because Bernice was beside herself. So,
they sat in the waiting area, tense.

"Mrs. Thomas?" The doctor had walked up to them.

Bernice sprung up from her seat, Marissa next to her.
"How is she?"

"She had a close call. It was good that the ambulance got
here on time. If she had delayed by half an hour, she would be
gone. Can I talk to you for a minute, Mrs. Thomas?"

"Anything you want to say, say it. We are all family here,"
Bernice replied. Dmitri, who had accompanied them, was also
listening in.

The doctor continued, "I have to ask you this: how long
has Gail been using drugs?"

This question threw them all off. Adonis looked at his
mother as she tried to make sense of the question.

"What do you mean, drugs?" she asked.

"The reason she had the seizure is because she suffered a mild overdose of OxyContin," the doctor replied.

"How… How is it possible?" Bernice was shaken.

"I think you need to ask her that when she regains consciousness. We have to keep her and then tomorrow we will assess how she's doing."

"Can I see her?" Bernice asked.

"Yes, but I can only let one person in for now."

Adonis nodded at Bernice.

"You go first, Ma. We'll wait out here."

Bernice left with the doctor. Adonis stood there, trying to process things. He needed to move.

"Damn," Adonis cursed under his breath.

"At least we know she's okay now," Dmitri said, seeking to comfort his friend.

"Yeah, but drugs? Since when?" Adonis asked.

"Hey, get your mind off it. She needs you guys to be positive for her. Okay? Want a soda?" Dmitri asked.

Adonis paused for a minute before nodding. "You want one, Marissa?" he asked. She shook her head.

"I'll get you a juice box," Adonis offered anyway. She didn't protest.

Adonis and Dmitri walked to the dispenser machine located down the hallway.

"Sorry about this," Dmitri said.

"It's all good. She's the last person I would expect to do that. She's too full of life," Adonis said.

"There were no signs?"

"Nothing out of the ordinary. This will hit my Ma on a different level."

They paused as they waited for the last soda to pop out.

"Look, now that you have graduated, and the internship is almost over, how about we go and build the dream we started?" Dmitri suggested.

Adonis sighed. "Yeah, it is an option for sure."

"But?"

"I sat there thinking about the hospital bill and everything. It made me want to talk to the boss at Sephtis first, see whether he has something for me," Adonis replied.

"Are you sure?"

"Yeah, I'm sure. Business can be flaky, man. You know how it is. I'll need the stability as we figure things out at home."

Dmitri nodded. "I hear you. The door here will always be open."

"I know."

As they walked back, Dmitri added, "You've got the sauce to make it there. Just watch out for the sharks."

"Sharks huh?"

"Yep. They are always there. If you look closely, you'll be able to see their fins pop out of the water before they strike. Just keep your eyes open."

CHAPTER TWO

THE RAY OF light streaking from the window hit Adonis's face as a thin streak at first, then got bigger as the sun rose. This made him fidget but wasn't enough to wake him from his slumber. He had spent the night at the hospital, watching over Gail in her ward. The hospital didn't allow visitors to stay overnight, but his mother stepped in saying, "It's either him or me." Fortunately, the doctor on duty allowed him to stay. Gail was still unconscious, her state prolonged through sleep-inducing medicine to keep her rested.

"Adonis, you are still here?"

Bernice walked in, carrying a bag. She shook him awake, and his eyes fluttered open.

"Hey, Ma," he said in his sleepy voice as he gathered his wits.

"Why is your phone off?" She had tried to call him, then

figured he might still be at the hospital and decided to come anyway. They had agreed he would be home early to change before leaving for work.

"It died. I forgot to ask you to leave me with your charger," he said, wiping his eyes. "What time is it?"

"It's seven thirty-five."

"Oh, fu—" he caught himself before he could swear, leaping to his feet. He went for the door.

"Need some clothes?" Bernice asked, as she took out a smaller bag from her luggage. He saw it and smiled.

"Thanks. Let me hit the washroom!" He dashed out.

Bernice walked over to Gail and stroked her hair, which was ruffled. A tear rolled down her left cheek.

🖌

Adonis ran out into the already hot bustling streets of the capital, Verdue. The streets were alive with people heading to work, but they were not congested. Even on weekdays, the streets looked like a summer vacation. Hawkers were stationed selling their fare as he darted this way and that. The office was going to be a twenty-minute ride by bus, but the ones he needed to catch were down the street. He got to the little terminus just as a bus got full and left. Another was getting in line. These were big buses, and would only leave when full, which was a half hour of waiting he could not afford. His mind raced as he looked up and down the street for an option. Did he have enough cab money? His stash was at home; the answer was no.

He spotted a rider at the corner of his eye and hailed him. He came over and they agreed on a reasonable fare.

So, for the first time he rode to work on a two-wheeler,

arriving fifteen minutes past the hour. He ran up the stairs to the fifth-floor offices of Sephtis. As he walked in, he could see through the glass what looked like a staff meeting. He slowed down and walked in as discreetly as possible. Gunner spotted him, giving him a disapproving eye. All the staff were gathered in the open plan office, listening to Vernon, who seemed to be giving a speech.

†

Vernon had seen Adonis walk in, but he had learned to hide his reaction towards things that irritated him. In his younger days, he would have stopped his speech, and fired him on the spot. But this was a different time and place. He had other battles to fight today, and an intern was not one of them.

He had arrived at 6:00 a.m. and opened the office himself. The guards were surprised, because his usual arrival time was 7:30 a.m., but he had things to attend to. Things that would change the course of Sephtis Entertainment and make it the global giant it was destined to be.

His father, the former real estate mogul whose wealth he had inherited and expanded into a large conglomerate, had once said that flipping the norm is what gets you ahead. Don't be familiar, get unfamiliar. The early bird may catch the worm, but it's more powerful when the worm catches the bird; the underdog taking on the giant is what makes champions. Vernon had done what he needed to do in real estate; that ship practically runs itself although he kept tabs on the operation. He now wanted a fresh challenge, and the challenge was found at Sephtis Entertainment.

Another secret his father shared was to inspire people to

wage war for you. Once you have their eyeballs on you, win their hearts and minds. Give them a rallying call and watch them make you money. It had worked well for him over the years.

So, after his morning bodyweight workout, he freshened up. At 8:00 a.m. sharp, he told Gunner to gather all the staff.

"Most of you have been here for the past four years since I bought this company, and we have made a lot of changes. This is not how it looked."

He clicked the remote control in his hand and the large LED screen showed the image of a drab regular brick and mortar office picture, with brown chairs, brown desks, brown floors – everything brown.

"That was the office I walked into four years ago. I thought to myself, 'this is a great place to rebuild!' I loved the place, partly because it has had a lot of great artists on its roster over the years. The other reason is because the founder, Ben Yates, won me over with his passion for music. He had built a great family here, and I wanted to give that work an extra boost. Which brings us to today. Look around you. See the colors, appreciate how far you have come. I didn't do this alone. You guys have brought value to this place and I am happy you let me do that."

He paused as his smiling listeners clapped in approval. He was glad to be making a connection.

"So, as part of our growth strategy, I am going to be launching two products. The first one will go into market as soon as next week, because we have the firmware and software ready to roll out. We introduce to you The Sephtis VIP Experience, where our higher end clients will be able to attend concerts of their choice with artists from our roster from anywhere in the world. Of course, at a nice fee, with customized VR headsets that will have tongues wagging a little."

As he said this the large screen paraded an exciting video of a well-to-do woman on her verandah, wearing a gold-plated headset with the Sephtis logo. The angle then changed from her exterior to the view of what she was watching: the exhilarating colors, sounds, and presence of Oceania doing her thing on stage.

The crowd wowed and then clapped with excitement.

"And the second product in our lineup is the one that will really blow people's minds."

Vernon paused as he built up their anticipation.

"This is yet to be named, and I might ask you all to suggest some good names for it, but just know that very soon people will buy smartphones that can project a *hologram* of their favorite performer. Yes, a hologram. Here's what I am talking about."

He clicked the remote again, and on the screen was a young man talking on a smartphone. He then hung up. He pressed its screen twice then placed it on the breakfast table. Two seconds later, the hologram of Oceania appeared, looking as realistic as ever, save for the fact you could see right through her. She was performing with the same energy as the VR image they had seen earlier, and the sound was fantastic.

People gasped, folded arms, looked at each other, held mouths agape – you name it. Then the claps started, and these ones were a bit longer than the previous, possibly because it was so revolutionary. Vernon was pleased with himself. *When they own it, they will run with it and make it successful.*

"This is the vision I am selling to you. All I ask is that you run the race with me. So, who's with me?"

The claps transitioned to shouts of 'Yeah!' and more fervent claps as everyone present raised their hands in the air.

"We will be winning. There will be a lot of winning!" Vernon shouted as he smiled widely, basking in the excitement that was now palpable in the room. The place was electrified. His eyes rested on the face of Adonis, who was clearly astounded by what he had just seen. His claps were not as energetic, perhaps in a daze from what he had just seen.

"Allow me to interrupt the early celebrations," Vernon began, marking the cue for the dying down of the claps and cheers. It went cool again, though the fizz was still there. "This won't take off without a team to work around it. I will count on all of you, and I ask you to give a lot of support to Leroy and the whole team that are working directly with FFX AI. And now, I will use this moment to introduce you all to a new member of that team."

He paused. Eyes and ears were pricked.

"Adonis Thomas, welcome to Sephtis Entertainment!" Vernon announced, letting every word land as he stared at the young man. "I am sure you have all seen Adonis around here running around during his internship. Well, he is now going to be a full-time employee here and part of the family. Let's all give him a hand for the good work that has got him here." Vernon led them in clapping for Adonis, who looked slightly bewildered.

"Adonis will join the FFX AI team from today, so after this meeting make sure you connect with Leroy. That's been a great start to the day. Thank you all. Let's get to it!" Vernon waved everyone away, and the crowd disintegrated as people headed to their workstations, murmurs and laughs filling the air.

A lot of people walked up to Adonis and patted him on the back.

"Congratulations, glad to have you around some more!"

"Good stuff, man! Go for it!"

Adonis was still showing his appreciation to all and sundry when Leroy walked up to him and shook his hand.

"Congratulations," Leroy began. "Just a heads up, you are going to be my first ever assistant. I enjoy working alone, so this will take some getting used to. Come, I have things to show you."

With that, Leroy completed introducing himself and was already heading to his office. Adonis quickly followed.

⚑

The FFX AI room was a haven. It was accessed through its own unique corridor that was lined from floor to ceiling with thick expensive carpet. The carpet reminded Adonis of the one in Vernon's office. He felt like he was desecrating it with each step he took.

"Just be careful that your shoes don't have silly dirt when coming here every morning," Leroy remarked, as if he had read Adonis's mind.

Next to the thick padded door was a fingerprint door lock, which opened once Leroy placed his finger on the scanner.

"They will enter your fingerprint in the system once you sign the contract. Come on in."

The office spacious and futuristic. The plush carpet continued here, lining the whole floor. On the walls were futuristic pieces of art that made you dream of other worlds, and posters of classic space-themed films done years ago such as *Gravity* and *Interstellar*. It was less colorful than the other spaces, but it didn't need it. The air-conditioning system was essential considering there were no large windows – the only two present were circular bulls-eye windows akin to portholes on a ship. They were airtight and were there to remind you there's still a world to go to outside.

There were four workstations, all spread apart to look like a space launch command center. Two computers were placed side by side with huge screens. Keypads with touchscreen capability were positioned below the monitors.

"Are these Genesys 800s?" Adonis asked in amazement.

"They're 1200s actually. They are not out yet because the specs are a bit too pricey for mass production. You get them on order. It's similar to how hard it was for people to order a Bugatti Centodieci supercar back in the day. You have to know how to get on the list and Mr. Wilson has the connections to make that happen. Have a seat."

Adonis sat into one of the well-designed bucket seats, like a rally car seat but with a healthy amount of padding. You fit snugly into it and focused on your machine, and Adonis found it quirky. He had a feeling Leroy was a gamer, but he didn't want to broach the topic.

As the computer came to life, the screen came alive with a simple minimalistic interface that invited you to explore it. Adonis's heart rate was increasing; he had done long conversations with Dmitri about Genesys supercomputers, but he had never thought he would be so close to one.

"One thing with this version is if you don't want to use touchscreen, you can activate motion mode," Leroy said.

"Motion mode?"

"Yeah, watch."

Leroy pressed a button on the top edge of the keypad and then hovered his finger over the screen without touching it. He swept his finger to the left and the file moved with him, placing itself in a folder at the other end of the screen.

"Wait – so it has motion sensors that track your movement?" Adonis asked in excitement.

"The movement of your assigned finger, yes. So, you can move files and open folders or type in without touching anything," Leroy said, moving some more files around. He clicked one file and it opened the hologram video that Vernon had shown them.

"These are going to be our babies. We are here to do something very special with this," Leroy said, clearly excited by the new advancements. He had the enthusiasm of a boy in a toy store.

This had clearly rubbed off on Adonis. "Man, this is just awesome! It's like the planets aligned for me to be here. I can only imagine how this launch will make Oceania's career blow up. She's so good!"

"Yes, she is," Leroy said then sighed. "I wish she was here to see it too."

"Wait, what do you mean?" Adonis asked.

Leroy turned to him. "You don't know?"

"Know what?"

"Oceania died in a car accident last week. She drove off a cliff into a small valley. Her funeral took place yesterday."

"No. No, you are joking, right?"

Suddenly the room was darker and chilly as Adonis tried to understand what he had just heard.

CHAPTER THREE

THE REST OF the day was a blur for Adonis. He was a mixed bag of feelings: wanting to celebrate a milestone in his career while mourning a gifted young woman he once knew. Granted, they were not friends in the strict sense of the term – Oceania was one of the most difficult people he had ever met – but she was always genuine, even in her flawed moments. He had not lost anyone he had closely interacted with recently, so her death came with a strong sense of loss. He knew she was going to be a star. She already was, snatched at the cusp of greatness.

That was his mood over lunch when his mother called to say they were going to discharge Gail. He didn't need to go. It was something else to be grateful for, and he looked forward to seeing her that evening. He didn't tell his mother about the promotion; it felt out of place to mention it.

When he got home later that day, he found them waiting for him to get home so that they could eat together.

"I thought it would be nice to have dinner as a unit now that Gail is back home," Bernice beamed, as she laid a bowl of spicy seafood on the table. Adonis was not really hungry but was glad to see his mother in good spirits.

Gail walked in from her bedroom with Marissa in tow. She looked frail but managed to flash a smile.

"Hey, Fireman."

"Hey, Princess. How are you feeling?"

"My guts still hurt. Maybe from the hospital thing but I figure it's also because I hate them," she joked. They both laughed. It was good to know her dark humor was alive and well. He also wondered if she was just feeling the effects of the medicine or suffering from withdrawal. The next few days would be intriguing.

"I'm sure the food can do some healing to them insides. Have a seat, honey," Bernice said.

They sat down to a warm dinner, although Gail was taking it easy on the portions. Adonis's appetite came back, and he dug in.

"So, did you survive the day?" Bernice asked.

Adonis wondered if his mother was asking about much more than the obvious. "Excuse me?"

"You were late for work."

"Still can't believe you slept in on a hospital chair," Gail said.

"Don't start, Gail,' Adonis said. "It's a pretty cozy hospital with its colors and all. I slept like a baby."

"I had to bring him a change of clothes. Did you get to shower?" Bernice prodded.

"I doubt it, considering the hug he just gave me," Gail said scowling.

"Go easy on him, Gail, he's only been here half an hour," Marissa protested.

"You were smelling the scent of success. Because believe or not, I got the job!" Adonis announced.

"You got what? You are hired full-time?" Bernice asked, excitement dancing on her tongue.

"Yeah, full-time with benefits."

The table came alive with a celebratory mood.

"I told you the good Lord wouldn't let you down. See now!" Bernice said smiling widely.

"Congratulations, mister! You still got that Midas touch," Gail said, with a cheeky wink.

"He never lost it, Gail. Never doubt this ninja," Marissa added lightheartedly. Gail poked her ribs for the jibe, Marissa wincing amid her smile.

Adonis sat back and basked in their flattery, enjoying it all. It had been a long time since he felt such warmth over an evening dinner. He was blessed.

When his sisters turned in, Adonis stayed up talking to Bernice. She was doing the dishes as he rinsed them off. She was the type of mother who believed that her children needed to be resourceful in the home, so he had been brought up on a culture of chores and helping out where he could.

"Did you guys talk when she got home?" Adonis asked.

"I didn't want to push her too much. She's been through a difficult two days, so I started easy. I asked her what happened.

She told me she had a stash on her. She had it for anxiety attacks she says. Since when did a graduation give anyone an anxiety attack, Addie?" Bernice asked. She wasn't buying it.

"Yeah, sounds like an excuse," Adonis replied.

"It is an excuse. So, I got a little angry, and said some harsh things to her. She deserved it because you can't do something like this to us. You have pressure? Talk! You have some stress? Talk to me! Since when do you use my money to buy yourself drugs? Not in my house you don't! I just regret the fact that I never saw it coming. It hurts to know that your daughter is keeping secrets she can't share with you," she said with a sigh.

"I hear you, Ma."

"Let's not talk about that now. At your new role, what exactly will you be doing?" she asked.

"I'll be working in their tech wing. Artificial Intelligence."

"What's that?"

"If I try to break it down right now you will get lost. Just know that it's a new technology that makes computers do things other computers cannot do," he replied.

"And can you keep up with that?"

"Yeah, I'm learning every day. I wish I could keep learning at home, but I will get the hang of it."

"What do you need? You know I am ready to—"

"No, Ma. You have sacrificed enough, and I don't know how to pay you back. I got this. It's time to focus on the two young ladies getting somewhere now," he said.

Bernice smiled. "That's why I call you my husband, you know."

"Slow down, Ma. I think we need to rethink that. It's going to add more pressure."

They both laughed.

Adonis didn't sleep well that night. However, he was surprisingly alert the next day despite being sleep deprived. He took his breakfast quickly and left earlier than normal. Leaving early meant he could walk to work. He liked walking through the old part of the city, which fortunately was along his route to the office. Here, the old buildings calmed him somewhat with their coral-stone walls and dated designs. He imagined things were less hurried then, so everything had to be intentional. Also, rough edges didn't take away from the charm of the building. Monuments to heroes of the revolution greeted him as he went along, keeping to the shade away from the glare of the rising sun.

As he neared the office, he realized the fog had not risen. He needed to talk to someone. He scrolled through his phone book and found a message on Face to Face, a dating app he had downloaded recently. He was a flirt. It stimulated his mind in new ways, the idea of connecting with a stranger virtually. He rarely ever wanted to hook up with one in person, but he had been chatting up this girl called Donalyssa, and the energy was crazy. So, when he saw her message, it brought a smile to his face.

"Where you at, big boy?" the text read.

"Headed to work," he texted back.

As he waited, he got the reply: "I have my people looking out to sea this morning."

Corny as it sounded, it was the coded flirt language he enjoyed with her. No expectations of perfect imagery.

"My cruise ship can come close to your dock and wave a salute," he replied.

"Sounds like a plan. What time do you want to sail by?"

He still had forty minutes to official work hours to kill, and he was one street away from getting to the office. He paused for a moment to think, then texted her back: "The tide is good right now. Meet at the seaside café in fifteen." It was close to her place, in case of anything.

When he met her, he knew they were going to get intimate. She was beautiful, with short curly hair, wide eyes, and a dimpled smile. Her lips were full, and she was curvy just the way he liked them. As they sat down to a quick coffee with bites, their flirtatious exchange was the same. They didn't finish their coffee. Her place was five minutes away. It was quick but intense, a frenzied session from two people who had raw desire for each other.

When he left her apartment half an hour later, Gunner had already tried calling him. He called back as he upped his walk pace.

"Good morning sir, I—"

"This is your second day in a row when you are running late. Give me a good explanation why that is the case," Gunner demanded.

"I—I have been having a situation with my sister. She suddenly fell ill, and we have been working through that." Technically, it wasn't a lie. Whatever drove him to do a hookup that morning wasn't the usual. "I'll be there in a few."

"As soon as you get here come to the meeting room," Gunner hung up.

Maybe it was the release from the hook-up session, but he was not anxious about anything. At all.

When he got into the meeting room, Adonis realized he wasn't going to be meeting Gunner alone. There were three other employees in there, including Russ, who was still an intern. Angie and David were the others in the room. Gunner was at the foot of the table, while everyone else flanked the sides.

"Finally, he arrives."

"I'm sorry I am late," Adonis said.

"I hope you are because I am this close to giving you a warning letter, and you have hardly been here a week," Gunner said, making a clipping gesture with his two fingers.

He knew Gunner meant business. It wasn't the right way to start your dream job.

"I was telling your colleagues here that we are going to have some visitors today. Clients that we have signed on to work on projects. So, we are expecting four people in an hour or so who want to see how we do things. We are here to sell them the dream, aren't we?"

"Yes, we are," everyone replied in unison.

"Good. So, of course, I need some help with this, and you guys know the lay of the land in this office and are good with people. You will be their chaperones. Adonis, you are familiar with what that is, right?"

"Yes, sir," Adonis replied.

"Good. Glad to see you all look presentable. So, let's meet at the reception in an hour, unless there are any questions."

Russ raised his hand.

"When you say clients, you mean—"

"Musicians. Artists. People who we have discovered and want to make best-selling records with. Three of them are amazing rappers, and one of them is a fantastic singer. I'll make introductions once they get here. Anyone else?"

No other questions were asked, and Gunner ended the meeting.

"Stay on, A.D."

Adonis didn't stand as the others left. The room was quiet and a little tense.

"Do you know why you are here?" Gunner asked.

"Yeah. I think so."

"I don't think so. Because if we shared the same aspirations to make you one of the best, then you wouldn't be coming here late two days in a row."

"I apologize. It won't happen again."

"No more apologies. You've run out of them. You haven't earned the right to walk up here anytime you want. Next time you want to do that, call me the night before. Otherwise, I will make sure you don't work here again. Am I clear?"

"Yes, boss."

Gunner grit his teeth. "I told you not to call me that."

Adonis had run out of apologies, so he bit his tongue. Then something came to him.

"Gunner, can I ask you something?"

"It better be good."

"I heard that Oceania died last week. It surprised me. What—Is there anything those who knew her can do?" Adonis asked in the sincerest tone possible.

Gunner paused, mellowing his stance. "You heard that huh? Sad story. We are doing something for her family as a company. Don't worry, we have a way of handling this kind of thing. Leave it to us, we'll sort it out."

"Okay. Thanks," Adonis said. He headed straight to the FFX AI office and spent the next hour learning new terms and shortcuts of the system with Leroy. He was still struggling to get through it, and time flew by so fast he was almost late again.

"Leroy, I have to run. Gunner needs me."

"I know, he told me. Go, do your thing"

"Thanks."

Adonis was the first at the reception, and the rest joined in. Shortly afterwards, the four artists walked in led by the swaggering Gunner.

"Welcome to your new home of creative expression, Sephtis Entertainment," he bellowed, filling the space with his enthusiasm. The chaperones all smiled and shook hands with the artists.

"Before we go too far, let me make introductions," Gunner said, proceeding to introduce his team by name first, with a brief but glowing description for each of the chaperones.

For the artists, he introduced the three rappers: Randal aka Randy Rah, a male rapper with a gold shock of hair; Bruce the Bermuda Triangle, a hulking young man with a metrosexual trim; Francine Mirrors, a young female rapper who actually looked like a librarian with her glasses and flowing hair; and finally Chanel Carter, a beautiful full-lipped singer with a fit body and a lazy gaze.

"Now that we all know each other, shall we begin the walkabout? Come with me," Gunner said, leading the way.

As they filed away, Adonis studied their gaits. His years of clubbing and connecting with artists had made him develop the habit. Simply put, he could tell who was a natural performer and who wasn't. Out of them all, he was drawn to Chanel's prancing gait; it was confident and sassy in its own right.

She caught him staring at her, as if she had a sixth sense for these things. He almost looked away but the gaze she gave lingered a bit, as if inviting him to look some more. She smiled with her eyes, the mark of a woman who knew what she carried.

He liked her already.

CHAPTER FOUR

GUNNER STARED AT himself in the mirror of the men's washroom. He had locked it from inside, although he could hear someone try the lock every few minutes. He had unbuttoned his shirt, exposing a bare chest with a little hair on it. His right hand was tracing a six-inch scar on the left side of his chest. It was still sore but healing well.

He didn't like getting these kinds of marks when doing the job. With DNA and advances in forensics, it was bad for business. But when he called the cleanup crew after he had killed her, they made sure nothing could be traced back to him. They didn't tell him what they did to her nails, the specific ones that dug up his skin as he choked her to death. It didn't matter. It was done.

They had wiped down her apartment, avoiding the usual mistakes that plague amateurs. No bleach, no footprints, no hair. The wipe down was an actual wipe down. The benefits of having the money to buy the best tech and people in the field was that the work was always professional.

It wasn't easy driving a car off a cliff in the night, so another crew had to come in and check out her car. It was a new one that he had ordered for her soon after the tour was over. She had wanted more money and some extra pampering, and to be honest she had earned it all. The tour was a resounding success, one of the best they had ever done. He was proud about how they had put it together and run a tight ship, despite the mild discontent she had shown on the road.

As soon as the car was ready, someone drove it to the chosen cliff, which was close to the party circuit she loved going to. He had entertained her earlier with a few drinks and some weed as they talked about the next steps, so her system was that of a typical partygoer who shouldn't be driving.

He was fascinated with how she was placed ever so carefully into the driver's seat, so realistically it felt like she was alive again. It had been less than an hour since her last breath, so maybe he was stretching his imagination a bit. The car accelerated down the road, hit the barrier at the exact weak point they had identified. Its momentum was sufficient to carry it headlong into the valley below. In the darkness, they could hear the crunching noises of metal on rock getting farther and farther away from them, until it stopped.

It was never an easy thing, sleeping after that. So, he found solace in listening to her music, over and over again until sunrise. He felt like he was making peace with her, like they were friends again. It helped him treasure the amount of work they put in over the many months. It was not in vain. This was not the end.

This was a new beginning for her, because music never truly dies. It keeps living in the people who listen to it for years after its creator is gone.

As he buttoned up his shirt again, he breathed in and smiled. He was getting better. His past haunted him, but the music was going to make it better. Music makes things better.

He started whistling as he walked out. He kept it going as his whistling and footsteps faded away until all you could hear was the occasional drip of water from a faucet.

↑

Adonis heard Gunner whistling and watched as he emerged from the corridor that led to the washrooms. Adonis and the artists were having a tea break after touring some of the office spaces. Sephtis had laid out quite the array of snacks. Alongside coffee, tea, and hot chocolate were sausages, sandwiches, crackers, buns, cookies, and cakes. It would give a good sugar rush for the rest of the tour. Adonis wondered if the visitors preferred shots of vodka from the office bar instead, despite the fact it was still morning.

Before they broke for tea, Gunner had charmed them through the various facilities on offer at the office: the retro-style meeting rooms for serious conversations, as well as the more relaxed hangout rooms with unorthodox furniture where brainstorms could happen. He introduced the artists to various department heads just for formality's sake. Adonis thought they would also meet Vernon, but that did not happen. Instead, Gunner took them to the two music recording studios. Tastefully designed, they were spacious and heavily soundproofed. Since quality does not come cheap, they had pricey state-of-the-art kit. Two of the best music producers-turned-sound engineers in the islands, Chaz and Ebony, were hired full-time to work their magic.

"You know not many people get in here. This going to be something you've never experienced before. I think you guys were born with music inside of you. We are here to get that juice out and share it with the world," Gunner said in an oratory manner. He was keen to make these newbies connect with reality as soon as possible.

While at the second studio, Gunner flaunted some musical instruments to them.

"We are in the business of working with musicians instead of digital artists who work with playback all the time. To reinforce this, we have a core group of instrumentalists we work with. You will meet them sometime down the road. Oh, and just to spice it all up, if you cannot play an instrument, it will be a good idea to start thinking about one," Gunner said.

Along one wall were two acoustic guitars, a bass guitar, a set of drums, two keyboards, a flute, and a saxophone. As the group was moving out of the studio, Chanel lingered near the acoustic guitar, feeling its grooves and edges.

"Hey, we are headed out," Adonis called to her.

Chanel did not react for few more seconds, before turning and heading for the door. As she went past, she whispered, "Nice guitar."

He could not tell if she was being sarcastic or defiant.

With the tea break done, they went to the upper floor of the office. It was sizeable and housed the other creative arm of the company: videographers, video editors, drone operators, graphic designers, and the marketing team. It was mostly open plan, with a colorful set up and the trademark unorthodox furniture to stir the creative juices. After a casual introduction to the team there, the artists followed Gunner into the film studio. It was a large room with green screen on one wall. Lights hung down from the struts that ran across the ceiling. There was a singular camera with two crewmen, but Adonis knew there was more equipment and personnel when needed.

"This is where we make the people love how you look. We are painters for your music, and you are the canvas – and we are very good at filming videos. So, as you do your music, think of the images you want to see in them. It's part of the journey," Gunner said.

Gunner then had them do an impromptu video shoot, allowing them to do random actions in front of the lens. Excited, each artiste took their time before the lens, doing monologues, freestyles, or jokes as their urges compelled them. Even Chanel lit up at this point, channeling her inner joker, Adonis thought. The whole session took close to an hour and a half.

Away from the film studio, there was a balcony with a view of one of the beaches. It had a few deck chairs and a pool table, possibly for employees who wanted to ease the stress of long work hours.

"Damn, this is dope as hell!" Randy Rah said, gesturing in wild excitement. He always seemed pent up with energy, Adonis noted, so he wasn't surprised.

"Yeah, when do we start?" Bruce added.

"Slow down! We haven't seen everything," Flavia cautioned.

"You have seen almost everything," Gunner said. "The rest will be experienced as you go along."

Adonis's eyes fell on Chanel, who was not chiming in. Casting a glance his way, she looked jaded.

"All right! Our resident chef has prepared a special lunch for us all. I will take you back to the cafeteria so that we can dig in. Also, feel free to talk to me, or one of my guys here. Sometimes I look like a tough guy, but my momma always tells me I am a good listener. Who am I to doubt her, eh?" he said with a smile, waiting for a reaction. Everyone laughed, save for Chanel who forced a smile.

At the cafeteria, there was a special VIP section for the guests, lined with cozy cream lounge chairs with tables next to them. After the artists settled in first, Gunner pointed out where his chaperones should sit, making sure they mingled with the artists to 'keep them busy'. As he led Adonis towards Chanel he whispered, "Get close to her. We need her to sign."

The artists chose a combo of seafood and chicken meals, with starters and dessert thrown into the mix. To top it off they got a cocktail from the office bar.

Half an hour later, everyone was having his or her meal amid loud conversation, while Chanel ate in silence.

"Enjoying it?" Adonis asked.

"I'm full," Chanel said. She had barely gone through half her plate.

"Are you sure?" Adonis asked. "There's ice cream for dessert."

"I'm lactose intolerant," she replied.

"All right then," he said, as he took another bite of his steak.

"Let's get out of here," she said.

"Where to?"

"How about the studio?"

He was not sure it would be open, but with Gunner on his case, he had to play along.

They got to the second studio. It was open. They had it to themselves, the engineer possibly on his lunch break. Chanel picked up the acoustic guitar and sat on the sound engineer's chair. Her fingers caressed it for a moment, and then she started playing.

Adonis heard the random strumming of notes build up into a soulful melody. Chanel closed her eyes, her whole frame embodying the rhythm of what she was playing. Adonis could have asked her to sing, but he did not want to ruin the moment. He found himself smiling, and as the tune hit its crescendo, Chanel opened her eyes, and their eyes locked. He was connecting, and she clearly loved that fact. She faded out the notes gently.

"You play it beautifully," he said.

Chanel took back the guitar to where she found it. She then walked back to him and said, "Cool."

They walked out together, smiling and in good spirits.

"Adonis, where have you been?" Leroy asked as he bore down on them. Adonis's smile disappeared.

"I was working with Gunner," he replied.

"I can see that! How far are we with the algorithm report?"

"Um, I haven't really had the time to look at it today," Adonis said.

"I suggest you make the time, because I need it in the next hour," Leroy replied, and walked off.

Chanel smiled in mild amusement.

"I will find my way to the gang," she said.

"Before I go, let me say this: you are the most gifted of that gang, and—"

Chanel cut him off by putting a finger over his lips.

"You try too hard. It doesn't look good on you," she said. With that, she walked off.

"Fucking idiot," he cursed under his breath. He wanted to go after her and redeem himself, but he knew it was futile. Resigned, he headed towards the FXX AI office.

Adonis buried himself in his work, studying the elements of the AI algorithm. Something was missing in his assessment, and he needed help. He would not ask the angered Leroy; it would make him look like he lacked focus.

"Are you done yet?" Leroy asked as the deadline inched closer. Adonis took a deep breath.

"Sir, first I apologize for earlier. I was in the wrong. I do not take this job for granted. About the report, I am still trying to figure this thing out. Could I get more time please?" Adonis asked.

Leroy, still pissed, ran his fingers through his hair. "All right. How much time do you need?"

"The next two days at least. If that's okay with you."

"That's fine with me. You can take the rest of the afternoon off, get some rest," Leroy said.

Adonis figured he got off early so that Leroy could cool off, but he did not mind. He felt like he had crossed a bridge there. The fact that Leroy had given him more time meant that he saw some potential in him. He smiled.

It was as he was walking out that he heard the distant shouts of excitement coming from upstairs. Curious, he went up the steps.

At the studio was the photographer, his crew of assistants and lighting technicians going through the paces. In front of them was the posing Chanel, painted with bright camera flashes every so often.

"Give me that seductive look... yes, with your head popping back a bit... beautiful!" the photographer directed as he moved around, getting the best angle before his camera clicked.

Adonis's eyebrows went up in surprise when he saw Chanel as she enjoyed her moment in the spotlight. She had no make-up but was still stunning. For some strange reason, he felt jealous that the photographer was able to direct her, making her smile, laugh or mellow at the drop of a phrase.

A hand fell firmly on Adonis's shoulder, squeezing it.

"You did well, A.D," Gunner said, "I don't know how you did it, but she took the deal."

"Nice! When?"

"Shortly after lunch," he replied.

Adonis smiled to himself, flashing back to the guitar session.

"Thanks."

"Don't thank me yet. There is still work to do. A full album to work on. When that comes out as a hit, then you can thank me," Gunner said.

"Great. When do they start working?"

"*We*. When do *we* start working, because you are now holding her success in your hands."

Adonis turned to Gunner. "What do you mean?"

"She's a hardhead, but she listens to you. So just make sure she comes through, and everything's going to be all right," Gunner said with a smile. Adonis could not tell if that was a threat or not.

Both men kept watching Chanel work it, with Gunner occasionally clapping in approval.

Adonis's phone rang. The photographer turned sharply to him.

"Get that shit out of here, you are messing with the flow!" he barked.

Adonis apologized and stepped out. It was his mother.

"Addie, where are you?"

"I'm still at work, Ma."

"I need you to come home," she said, her voice shaking, "Come home now."

"What's wrong?" he asked.

"It's Gail. She's on drugs again! Please come, because I don't know what to do!"

CHAPTER FIVE

ADONIS GOT HOME in fifteen minutes flat. He had left the studio without saying goodbye to anyone, his mind fixed on moving as fast as possible. He grabbed a cab that was idling outside the office. The mid-afternoon traffic was light. Still, the driver took the extra step of driving through the old part of the city, a shorter distance to home. Adonis appreciated this and tipped him.

When he got into the house, Adonis found his mother and sister standing over the couch. Gail was lying on her back, flat on the couch. She was smiling and talking to herself.

"Oh, thank God you are here! Your sister is going to send me to an early grave," his mother Bernice lamented. "Look! What is this? Why is she doing this to us, eh?"

"Relax, Ma, do we need to take her to hospital?"

"No, this isn't another overdose, but it could have been," Bernice replied.

"Tell me what happened," Adonis said.

"We woke up as usual, she was in good spirits. Nothing crazy happened. Then this afternoon Marissa finds her like this. Where did she get this garbage?" Bernice asked.

Adonis wondered too. They had cleaned out her room before she got out of the hospital. She either hid them very well or someone smuggled them in.

"I'll look into it," Adonis said. He watched his sister for moment. "Keep her lying there. I'm going to check her room."

"I already looked," Marissa said.

"I'm checking again," Adonis replied.

He got into her bedroom. The room was small for a teen, but their mother could not afford to move them to a bigger house. At least everyone had their own room. The walls were painted lemon yellow with pink bubbles just over her messy bed. Bedding lay crumpled across the bed, and there were dirt stains on her pillowcase.

He looked in between every item of bedding. He checked under her bed, in her bedside drawer, her closet, and even inside her shoes. Nothing. Then he noticed the packs of chewing gum. She had three different flavors atop the drawer, and one of them was open. He poured its contents onto his palm and amidst the gum pellets were two tablets of OxyContin. He ripped open the other two packs and came up with six more tablets of the drug. He returned the packs of chewing gum and took away the tablets.

He returned to the living room and found his mother and Marissa holding a bucket for Gail as she threw up.

"I found them," Adonis said, holding up the hand with the tablets.

"What are you going to do with them?" Bernice asked.

She instructed Marissa to keep hold of the bucket and walked up to him. "Show me."

He unclasped his hand and she examined them.

"I'll get rid of them," he said.

"Good. I can't have that crap under my roof!" she replied.

"Is the throwing up helping?"

"I hope so," Bernice replied as they turned to her. Gail looked like she was dozing off as Marissa adjusted the cushion under her head.

"Where do we take her?" Adonis asked.

"Nowhere. She stays here," she replied.

"I thought you wanted her in rehab?" he asked.

"I was wrong. She's my baby girl, she will just have to recover from home. What I need to do is find someone who can help us do that."

They stood in silence watching Marissa clean up.

"I can talk to Dmitri. He was a youth counsellor once. He's helped some with drug addictions before," he said.

"Are you sure?"

"I'm sure. Plus, he knows us, so we can trust him," Adonis replied.

Bernice turned to him. "What are you waiting for? Go talk to him!" she said, then headed to the couch.

Adonis left.

ⵓ

"I'm asking you because I trust you, and you won't let our business get out," Adonis said.

Dmitri took a sip of his coffee before nodding. They were

at a street café in Blue Lake. Adonis needed to get away from the house and clear his head.

"It's been a while though."

"Three years is not a long time," Adonis replied, "it's like riding a bike. Once you learn it you can't forget."

Dmitri laughed. "I guess you are right. Pop them out, let me see them," he said.

Adonis looked around the café before taking out the tablets. He hid them from view with his upturned palm as Dmitri studied them.

"Brings back memories," Dmitri said.

"Are you talking about the youth camps or the sessions?" Adonis asked.

"You know what I'm talking about. Those escapades were legendary."

"Don't go there, Dimi," Adonis warned.

"I'm not. Just giving you a little throwback," he said, winking. "So, cold turkey?"

"Yeah. Ma does not want anything to do with rehab. You know what to do to ease her out. I don't think she is in too deep. At least I hope she isn't," Adonis replied.

"Early user can be easier to handle, so fingers crossed. When do we start?"

"We already did. I'm calling Ma to tell her you are coming in the morning."

Dmitri laughed. "Cool. What are you going to do with the rest? If the cops catch you with them it won't end well."

"Keeping two to see if I can find the dealer. Have to cut off her supply."

"Or the rest go to the singer crush?"

Adonis frowned, "Why bring that up now?"

"You can make things move faster with these. Give them to – wait, what was her name again?"

"Chanel. And you know I'm not like that anymore," Adonis replied.

"Give them to Chanel and ride the waves," Dmitri teased.

"Stop it, she's signed to the company, I can't mess up."

"What if she wants you to mess it up? In a good way. On the down low," Dmitri posed.

Adonis sighed. "Honestly. I wouldn't know how to act. She has those vibes that make me want to do crazy things. So, keeping the boundaries is a good thing."

"Hmmm, sounds like when I met my ex Carlos. Well let's hope the walls of Jericho don't fall!" Dmitri said, as he took another sip of coffee. Adonis could not help smiling as he dialed his mother.

↑

The next day, after making sure his mother and sister were primed for Dmitri's arrival, Adonis left for work. He arrived to find the place busy. The newly signed artists were doing what Gunner liked to call 'warm-up' recording sessions. They were recording sessions with each music producer to build a creative connection. The artist would know each producer's strengths, and the producer would be able to gauge the artist's range. Sessions were set to last for half an hour per artist, but this varied. You cannot rush art, Gunner would say. If sessions went over an hour, Adonis suspected that Gunner would be pleased because it usually meant there was going to be some good material. If it was not working, the session was shortened. Gunner wanted

Adonis to step into the sessions. Adonis knew this might bring friction again with Leroy, so he asked to join in later.

He got a break three hours later and joined in when Bruce the Bermuda Triangle was doing his session. He was in the recording booth, while on the other side of the transparent glass were the controls manned by Chaz, the music producer. Behind Chaz stood the watching Adonis and the seated Chanel, who was playing a mobile phone game.

Between the two producers, Adonis liked Chaz because of his carefree personality.

"She's smoking me out, vibe over vibe, giving me out, having the time of my life," Bruce free styled over a track. Chaz stopped the beat and looked into the booth.

"I'm still not feeling this! You wanna take a break?" Chaz asked.

"Nah, nah, I'll come good! Let's go!" Bruce said enthusiastically, as he patted down his slick hair. Adonis noticed the man was sweating, and possibly unsure of himself.

The beat came on again, and Bruce went for it.

"Ah ah ah, look into eyes and the sunrise, I got what you need and like, jamming with Chaz brings that vibe vibe."

Chaz stopped the beat again in irritation. Adonis rarely saw him like this, so he was amused.

"All right, enough! Get out, go for a walk, drink water or smoke something. I don't care. Just work on your craft!" Chaz shouted.

"Come on Chaz, I'm good, I swear," Bruce replied.

"No, you're not good! You have a decent voice, good delivery but whack lyrics. You can't freestyle for your life! We will get a good songwriter, and we will make hits with you. So, don't sweat it. You just can't freestyle!" Chaz said.

Bruce, a little shaken, went quiet for a moment. Chanel was smiling wryly, pausing her game to witness the exchange.

"It be like that huh?" Bruce asked.

"Yeah it be like that. It's called honest feedback. We are still gonna make a star out of you, don't let it get to your head or heart," Chaz replied.

Without a word, Bruce took off his headset. He walked out of the booth and went straight out of the studio to cool off.

"Chanel, you ready?" Chaz asked.

"Can I play the guitar?" she asked.

Chaz's eyes lit up. None of the artists had asked to play an instrument. "By all means!"

Chanel took the guitar and entered the booth. As she settled next to the recording mic, Adonis thought she looked like an angel as the overhead light simulated a halo on her hair.

She strummed the guitar, and another melodious tune came through. She did not sing this time; she simply spoke her soulful words over the guitar notes.

"I stopped crying when you walked through the door, and now I know that meeting you was never by chance," she began, going into her zone. Chaz was taken in immediately, his head bobbing as he savored her voice and skill. He turned briefly to nod his approval at Adonis, who gave him the thumbs up.

Chanel went on and when she hit her crescendo, she suddenly went quiet. She bowed her head, hugging the guitar.

"Are you okay?" Chaz asked.

She nodded as sniffles came through the microphone.

"I think you better get in there," Chaz said to Adonis.

Adonis entered the booth and walked to her. She looked up, tears rolling down her cheeks.

"What's wrong?" he asked.

"Can we go outside please?"

"But you are not done yet," he said.

"I'm done."

He did not insist, helping her up. Adonis handed the guitar to Chaz, who was wondering what was going on.

🌴

"Want to talk about it?" Adonis asked her, as he handed her some orange juice.

She took the glass and studied it for a few seconds. She was no longer crying.

"It's interesting how the best way to get juice out of a fruit is by squeezing, blending, or biting it. Don't you think?" Chanel said.

"There are different ways to make it I guess," he replied.

"But what's the one thing they have in common?" she asked. Her eyes locked with his, trying to read him.

"You tell me."

"Violence. They are all different types of violence. We get sweetness from a violent act," she said, as she sipped the juice.

"Is that what caused the reaction back there? Violence?" he asked.

"I don't want to talk about it, you know. It doesn't make me feel good about myself," she replied.

"You are one of the most talented people I have met. Yet, you are complex. Complex and beautiful," he said.

"What's your definition of beauty?" she asked.

"You are."

She paused, and then laughed. A loud laugh that appealed to him.

"You are not very good at this, are you?" she said.

"I am good at other things to make up for it," he replied.

"Like what?"

"Let me show you."

↑

They made their way back to her hotel room. They had barely closed the door when he spun her around. She waited for him as he moved closer and kissed her, gently. Her lips tasted just like he thought they would, soft and warm. She kissed back, and their lips kept searching each other, growing in intensity.

"Wait!" she said, after pulling away suddenly.

"What's wrong?"

"Come," she said, taking his right hand and leading him to the bed. She took off her top and threw herself on the bed.

Adonis paused for a moment. "Are you sure?"

She grabbed the front of his shirt and pulled him towards her. "Shut up and come here."

↑

Her head lay on his chest as they both caught their breath.

"That was... much livelier than I expected," she whispered.

"Livelier? That's the one word you use for it, *livelier*?" he asked.

"I'll rephrase. It was quick. But good enough to be the highlight of my day."

"I could feel a connection the moment you walked into the office, so I am not surprised."

Chanel suddenly pulled back. She lifted herself off his chest and started dressing.

"What?" he asked in bewilderment.

"Look, don't read too deep into this. It's a nice, one-time thing. I needed to refocus, and you've helped me do that," she replied.

"Are you serious right now?" he asked, also reaching for his clothes.

"It's best to just keep it real," she replied.

Five minutes later, he was walking back to his office. Alone.

↑

Leroy was looking at one of Oceania's performances when Adonis walked into FFX AI. He was still wrestling with his attraction to Chanel now that he was simply a quick hookup to her. He felt used, somewhat, which angered him. Donalyssa had left him feeling energized, and she was a quick shag. This was anti-climactic, and he hated it.

However, seeing any image of Oceania always sobered him up quickly. He was soon engrossed in watching her.

"She was a gift that comes around once in a lifetime," Leroy said.

Adonis nodded, and then a question came to him. "Leroy, how many artists have you worked on with this system?"

"About ten," he replied.

"Oceania was top of the list?"

"She's the crème-de-la-crème of all of them. Outstanding talent."

"Who were the others in the top five?

"Hmm. All right, so we are talking about great talent that also sold a lot of records for us. There are Flava and Derrick

Summers; they formed the group Sex Dungeon. The other two I would put there are Janice Peters and Teddy Campbell. Teddy was a great rapper too."

"Was?"

"Yeah. He went off the grid three years ago. No one knows where he is, although there were reports that he flew off the island to start a new life. We think he just quit music."

Adonis was curious. "Are the other artists still with us?"

"Janice is still with us. We have Sex Dungeon's music, but ever since Flava went missing, Derrick decided he doesn't want to record any new tracks."

"Hold on. You have two artists who went missing?"

"Hmm. Now that you put it that way, it does sound odd. Look, I do not know their stories too well. That aside, here's another thing I want you to add in your report," Leroy replied, as he switched back to the working interface.

Adonis was hardly listening. Something was not adding up.

CHAPTER SIX

WHEN ADONIS GOT home, Dmitri was just leaving. He escorted him down the street.

"How is she doing?" Adonis asked.

"It's been a long day," Dmitri said. "She started feeling the itch this afternoon, so that wasn't pleasant. Tried to keep her in check. She asked for a fix countless times. I know how to handle all that, but it takes time and energy."

"I hear you, and I respect you doing this for us. No other drama?"

"None. Let's hope that continues. Just watch her carefully tonight. How was yours?" Dmitri asked.

"Crazy. Had a lot to work on," Adonis replied.

"How's little mama doing?"

"She's good."

"Made a move on her yet?"

Adonis smiled sheepishly.

"Oh no you didn't!" Dmitri began, reading his friend's face, "You little shit! How was it?"

"Pretty dope. She liked it too. It was short though."

Dmitri nodded his approval, "Pent up energies huh? Nice! Now you gotta keep it regular if you like her."

Adonis shook his head, "Nope. Not happening."

"What, why not?"

"She's not into it," Adonis replied.

"Not into what? Banging or what?"

"Getting serious or looking like it could get serious," Adonis answered.

Dmitri laughed. "She played the one-night stand thing?"

"Yep."

"She's cold," Dmitri said, patting Adonis's shoulder, "but that doesn't mean the game is up."

"Oh, it's up. She's the type to make up her mind and keep it moving," Adonis replied.

"I guess you finally found your match," Dmitri said.

"What are you talking about?"

"You like to hit and leave, don't you?"

"That's not my play," Adonis protested.

"It's a different move, but the end is the same. You've done that plenty of times, hell even I have with Jimmy, Cindy, Luca, Hugo, Bianca, Martin, Desmond, Lisa even Paula and she had everything."

Adonis thought about it for a moment and had to agree. He had never gone steady with a girl in years. Casual flings were just less complicated. "Never thought it feels this messed up," Adonis said.

"Sorry to ruin your pity party, but you'll get over it. I have to go now. I have a bus to catch," Dmitri said, slowing down at the junction where they would part ways for the day.

"Wait, I am having a hard time figuring out some of the FFX AI. I'm supposed to come up with a theoretical analysis of how Sephtis's personality computing works. Got any references about neural networks I can check out?"

Dmitri got lost in thought for a minute.

"There's a group I want to introduce you. It's called Crab's Nest. It's an anonymous online community for nerds who talk shop about everything artificial intelligence. I'm sure you can find a discussion board about it, or you can just throw in your question. You have to be smart there though, never give out too much info to those guys. The people there operate from all sorts of places, including the dark parts of the deep web," Dmitri said.

"Hook me up, and I'll handle it," Adonis said.

"Thing is, you have to get someone to recommend you first."

"Why, you are not part of it?"

"Nah, not my thing. Some of those guys are high-level hackers, and they are paranoid about security. My brother knows a guy who's in it," Dmitri replied.

"Your brother? He who is part of a biker gang, knows guys in artificial intelligence?" Adonis asked.

"Calm down. There are a lot of things and people that Kai knows that would blow your mind. I'll leave it at that," Dmitri replied, "I'll get in touch with you later; see if he can hook you up."

"No worries. Thanks a lot for everything, I don't know how I'd get through this without you," Adonis said.

As Dmitri left, Adonis watched him for a few more minutes before heading back home.

He found Gail was already asleep after getting some sleeping pills, while Marissa and his mother were watching a movie. He took the dinner set aside for him and headed to his room.

Working on his computer, he used an encrypted browser and started searching. His conversation with Leroy was still nagging him. He needed to find out more about Flava and Teddy Campbell. First, he looked for Flava's actual name. It was not hard to find. There had been many news reports and features about Sex Dungeon's rise as a group. However, he was surprised that Flava was a young woman. Her legal name was Michaela Higgins.

Michaela Higgins and Teddy Campbell.

He followed a trail of news reports surrounding each one's exit from music. There was really nothing about Teddy Campbell, except a three-year-old report from his publicist, a certain Renée Palmer, to the effect that 'Teddy is retiring from music to focus on family. Let us respect his privacy at this time.' After that, nothing. He had more luck finding Michaela Higgins. He found a report of her disappearance two years earlier. There were even full-page ads taken out seeking to find her. There were no reports confirming that Michaela was found. Adonis found images and short mobile phone videos of vigils held in her memory. Then he stumbled upon her home address. He wrote it down, folded it, and stashed it in his wallet. He wanted to use it the next day. It was past midnight when he turned in.

↑

"Gunner tells me you had a special liking for Oceania," Vernon said.

He was sitting at his desk, reading something on his widescreen tablet. In front of him sat Adonis.

"She was an amazing performer. She had presence I had never seen before," Adonis replied.

"I couldn't agree more. Where do you think she could have gone with her music?" Vernon asked, leaning back in his chair.

Adonis paused briefly, and then replied, "After studying the trajectory of her numbers with Leroy, I have no doubt she was going to be the biggest star in the company."

"Good analysis. Now, that upward trajectory started when she was alive," Vernon said. "I think history shows that when an artiste of that caliber dies, the sales of their singles or albums, or even memorabilia, goes up. True?"

Adonis nodded. "Yes, sir."

"Oceania still has a lot of fans, and we want to keep her memory going. Something that sets us apart from the competition is that we work very hard to get our talent into the studio and recording as much music as possible from the moment they put pen to paper. We are now lucky – no, *blessed* – to have a good number of unreleased tracks done by Oceania. I feel one of the best ways to pay tribute to her memory is to launch a posthumous album. What do you think?" Vernon asked.

As Adonis watched the man speak, he began liking the idea more. He also could not shake off the truth that it was a money grab. They owned all her music and image rights. The company would make a good amount of money for years, far more than they had invested in Oceania.

"I agree. I think her fans and other people who recently learned of her will appreciate it. In terms of her pull with fans, I do not think it matters whether we release a single or an album. Her fans want to hear something new, and we can give it to them. In terms of revenue, releasing the album will bring in more. People will not just be buying her music. They will be building a collection."

"I like the sound of that. Since you've broken it down so well, I want to put you in charge of tracking that album's sales. Are you up for it?"

"Yes, yes I am! Thank you, sir. I'll give it my best shot," Adonis replied, smiling widely. It was a show of trust. Adonis had a spring in his step as he walked towards the FXX AI office.

"The report is due tomorrow, remember that?" Leroy asked.

"Yes, I remember," Adonis replied. Dmitri had not gotten back to him, so he sent a quick text reminding him about the Crab's Nest.

"Leroy, was there someone who used to work here by the name of Renée Palmer?"

"Yeah, she used to work here. Left early last year. Why?"

"I was just studying the artist roster and came across her name," he replied.

"She was a publicist, not an artist," Leroy clarified.

"Yes, that's right. Sorry about that," Adonis replied, as he settled into his seat. That was one more connection made, but where did it lead?

Lunch hour could not come fast enough for Adonis. Once the clock hit one o'clock, he avoided being strung to the canteen and hit the outdoors. He hailed a cab. As he settled in behind the driver's seat, he read the address he had written.

"Take me to 54 Macaulay Street," he instructed.

The street was in a middle-class part of town, lined with bungalows from end to end.

"There's house number 54," the driver said.

"Drive on a little more, going past it just a bit, and then park."

They stopped twenty feet from the house. Adonis watched it for a few minutes. It was a bungalow with a live fence surrounding it. There was no movement.

"You realize I am still charging you for waiting, right?" the driver asked.

"Yes. Please wait for me," Adonis said, as he left the cab.

He walked slowly to the house, just in case there were dogs around. He was not a fan. At the front door was a pink-colored bell. He rang it and waited.

The door swung open to reveal a woman in her fifties wearing a long bathrobe, a shower cap, and holding a brown mug.

"Yes, can I help you?" the woman asked with a deep throaty drawl.

"Sorry to bother you, am I at Michaela Higgins' home?" Adonis asked.

"Who's asking?" the woman asked with suspicion.

"My name is... Simon, and I was doing a story on her life. I was wondering if I could talk to you briefly?"

"I'm tired of doing news stories since none of you helped us," the woman replied.

"Sorry for your loss, ma'am, but I actually want to know what happened."

"After all this time, now is when you want to know what happened? Why didn't you publish it when we found her?"

"Wait, you found her?" Adonis asked, surprised.

"We found her months later. Or what was left of her," the woman replied, taking a sip of what Adonis figured was green tea.

"Where and how did you find her?" Adonis asked.

"An anonymous call. He—" the woman paused, holding

back emotion, "he said we should check the North Creek. So, we did. Her remains were there."

"I'm…. I'm so sorry to hear that."

"Autopsy said she fell off. An accident or something. I don't buy that for a minute, but what can I do? At least we got to bury her in a decent grave," she said, wiping away a tear.

His phone started ringing. He ignored it.

"Why wasn't it in the news?"

"I can only guess why, you know," she said, resigned. "Are you going to pick that up?"

He took out the phone. It was Dmitri. Adonis tried angling his phone to prevent the woman from seeing the screen name. He declined the call.

"I would really like to talk to you some more. Do you mind if I come by again?" he asked.

"Actually, I do. I do not want to talk about it. It only dredges up more pain. I also know that you are not a reporter. But whatever you are, don't come back. My family does not need more pain."

Adonis did not know what to say at that point.

"Thank you, Mrs. Higgins," he mumbled, as the door shut in his face.

🌱

As he walked back to the waiting cab, he called Dmitri.

"Sorry I couldn't pick your call. Is Gail okay?"

"Yeah, she's fine so far. She is not eating much though. Another day and she'll probably be getting back to herself."

"I hope so. What's up?"

"Check your email for the link. Your recommendation is by Marty C."

"Great! Thanks, man. Wait, before you hang up. You remember when I told you one of the artists I worked with here died recently, right?"

"Yeah."

"I discovered two artistes who disappeared in the past three years after getting signed. I did a little more digging and just found out that one of them died," Adonis said.

"What are you trying to figure out?"

"I wonder if it's a coincidence."

Dmitri cleared his throat. "Listen, people die all the time. Don't read too much into it."

"I know but—"

"No buts. Stop messing up your new job with this detective shit. Stay focused," Dmitri said.

"I guess you're right. Thanks," Adonis said, hanging up. He sighed as he got into the cab.

↑

When he got back to Sephtis, the receptionist pointed up towards the film studio. "You better head up," she said.

When he got there, he found Gunner in the middle of a speech.

"… And then at the end of the week we will review each video," he said, noticing Adonis's arrival, "so let me recap that for those who were not here: do a track on day one, master it day two, shoot the music video day three, edit the video day four, we screen the videos together on day five. *Capisce?*"

The heads in the room nodded, except one: Randy Rah's hand was up.

"With all due respect, for someone like me, I think all that is unnecessary," he said.

"How so?" Gunner asked.

"I'm not really up and coming. I have shot fifteen music videos just to get here. Some of them all on my own. I have paid my dues. I can step back from this week and let the rest do it."

Gunner laughed, rubbing his hands as he paced. Adonis knew the man was angry.

"I hear you. I hear you," Gunner said.

"Are you sure you hear me? Because you were laughing and that's not cool," Randy Rah said.

"I can laugh if I want. To answer your question or comment, the workflow is non-negotiable. You have to do it. It's in your contract," Gunner said.

"I'm not interested in wasting a whole week when I can write tracks," Randy Rah replied, holding up his notebook. Gunner's hand, in one deft move, hit the notebook across the room.

Randy Rah glared at him. Standing up, he squared up to Gunner, who was shorter.

"You may be my boss but you gotta treat me with respect!" Randy Rah shouted

"Step back!" Gunner warned.

"You should have—" Randy Rah began, but he did not get to finish what he wanted to say.

Gunner was impatient with indiscipline, and had made his move, crouching down. Randy Rah, surprised, leaned forward – and that was his big mistake. Gunner was already coming back up with an upper cut that connected with Randy's lowering chin. Randy Rah's body went limp. His knees buckled as he collapsed to the floor. He groaned, unable to move his limbs.

Gunner raised himself upright, standing over the fallen rapper. After staring at him, Gunner raised his head. His eyes seared with anger as he addressed the group.

"Listen to me very carefully. For the next few months, we will bust our asses to make you stars. But you will do it on our terms. Go and read your contracts, page by page, line by line. Learn this: I own you."

CHAPTER SEVEN

RANDY RAH WAS out for five minutes before he regained consciousness. He was taken to an emergency unit on the ground floor that Adonis never knew about. A small, three-room facility, it was kitted out handle outpatient emergencies. A doctor and her nurse manned it, so they attended to Randy Rah quickly. The following week, things ran like clockwork. Every artist on the roster towed the line, at least in public. They wrote their songs, with Chanel co-writing one for the hapless Bruce. They then recorded the singles and shot their music videos. Adonis was not able to be there for most of the sessions; he delivered his report to Leroy, who was impressed. The Crab's Nest forum had proved to be a boon for Adonis. He simply described the scenario he was looking at, giving zero personal information. The community came to his aid, helping him troubleshooting the gaps. He learned more about neural computing in one hour than Leroy had taught him since he started working there. Assignment done, Adonis worked hard to catch up with Oceania's current album sales in anticipation of the upcoming album.

Towards the end of the day, he passed by the edits and found each artist seated next to their editor. Except Chanel, who was nowhere to be seen.

"Where's Chanel?" he asked her editor. He simply shrugged.

"She went to the room for a nap," Francine said.

Adonis shook his head and checked the edit timeline. Shot on green screen, the video now had Chanel on a desert, walking the dunes. She was dressed in a figure-hugging outfit, a departure from all the loose clothes she normally donned. He appreciated that she looked good in anything she wore.

"How far are you with the edit?"

"I'll be ready for the final preview in ten minutes or so," the editor replied, "She'd better be here to sign off or Gunner will be pissed."

Adonis knew this might fall on him. He headed for the exit.

Outside, he walked to the nearby hotel where all the artistes stayed. It actually belonged to the company, but that was an unspoken truth. He walked into the reception and got her room number. Exiting the elevator on the fifth floor, he walked down the hallway. Room 1015.

He knocked. "Chanel! I know you are in there."

He heard movements and then the door opened. She left it open and walked off to the balcony, her flowing braids swinging in the breeze from the outside.

"You are supposed to be at the edits for your final preview," he said.

"You don't say?" she replied, holding up a glass of wine and taking a sip.

"Why are you acting like this?"

"Because I don't like this. This is not working for me," she replied.

"What is not working for you?" he asked.

"Everything. The orders, the punishing schedule, forcing me to wear skimpy stuff that only serves to objectify me, rewriting my lyrics to making this commercial instead of artistic... I mean, everything is so... so engineered, so factory-like," she lamented.

"But you are being prepared for the real world. Granted, Gunner can be a pain in the ass sometimes, but he is doing a good thing. He is toughening you up. This industry takes no prisoners, and it is not kind if you do not learn how to survive it. They are teaching you how to roll with the punches before you actually have to do it," he said.

"And then what? Die a robot? Become a cut-out of the artist I actually am?"

"No. Then thrive like a queen. You have to push extra hard when starting out so that you can reap the rewards later."

"Nah, this is messing me up. I'm not built for this," she said, shaking her head.

Adonis watched her for a moment as she stared at the traffic below.

"So what do you want to do?" he asked.

"I want to go home. I thrive when I am there. Let me create where I am most comfortable, I will send you guys the music. Chaz can do his thing because we click. Easy!" she said.

"You know that Gunner will never let that happen," Adonis said.

"Who gives a damn about Gunner? He can go play in traffic!" she said, as she strode back into the room. He followed her. She threw her suitcase onto the bed and started packing clothes from her closet.

Bemused, Adonis asked, "How do you expect to get out of here?"

"Through the front door," she replied.

"That's not going to happen," he said. "He's watching you from the moment you walk out that door. By the time you get downstairs with all that, they will be waiting for you."

"Then you will help me do it."

"Oh, hell no, Chanel. We are going to stay here and get through this."

"Over my dead body," she said, as she went on packing.

He moved to stop her. She fought him off for a short time and then gave in. He could have kissed her then, because her warmth and the richness of her scent drew him in. However, he held back.

"We will get through this. Trust me," he said. She hugged him for a few seconds, sniffling tears.

"Let's go finish that edit, okay?" he said.

She nodded. As he walked with her down towards the office, he realized he had sold her a dream whose outcome he deemed uncertain.

↑

"How would you feel if I said that I am talking to Terek?"

She slid in the question quite casually, but it still hit him like a bolt. This was not because he was angry that his mother was talking about their long-lost father, but that she was falling for his tricks again. Every time his father tried to reconnect, his mother became weak to the advances. His two sisters also saw him in a favorable light, despite the fact the man had been away from their lives for five years. Adonis simply saw through the bullshit.

"Are you talking to him?" he asked.

"Not yet. Just a thought."

"But it's not a thought you entertain often, so forgive me if I find it strange," he said.

"Strange or unsettling?" she asked.

"A bit of both then," he replied. "Why do you want to talk to him after all these years? And don't tell me it's because he is my father. That ship sailed away for all of us."

Bernice sighed. "He might be able to help out with Gail," she said.

Adonis turned to look at her. "Help her or ruin her?"

"He doesn't drink or do drugs anymore, so I hear."

"So, you hear? He's a very good actor, we both know that. Anyway, we have things under control. First off, Dmitri is doing a great job. Second, Gail is not a junkie. Her withdrawal is going fine so far, which means that she had not gone in too deep. We do not need him. He will make her worse," Adonis said.

"Dmitri can't do it forever. Besides, I would only want him to talk to her, nothing more," she said.

"We've been talking to him on phone calls and video calls when he chooses to be found, and we are doing just fine. Why do you want him physically here?"

"Some things need to be done face to face. Dmitri is not doing it on phone or online, right?" Bernice asked.

"And then when he leaves again, what will happen? When his next exit affects Gail, won't she go looking for a hit? No, Ma. That would be a mistake. So, forget about it please," he said in exasperation.

"Okay. I hear you, Addie, and you have a point. I … I guess it's fear that's making me think of ways – just new ways of dealing with this."

"It won't happen again, Ma. Trust me," he said. He kissed her on the forehead and headed for his room.

He could not sleep after that conversation. He went searching on the Web again: Teddy Campbell. He decided to change tact and look at it from the company angle. He struck gold when he found out that Sephtis had two other subsidiaries: Tetra Records and Nova Entertainment. Teddy was signed on to Tetra. Adonis found an online magazine feature under the artist moniker Teddy Flow. There, in the third paragraph, was the mention of where he grew up. Coronation Street. It did not take long for Adonis to find the exact address, and he jotted it down. Satisfied with his progress, he turned in.

🌴

The next morning, Adonis was walking to his FXX office when Chanel appeared and blocked his path.

"I need to show you something," she said.

Before he could reply, she led him up the balcony and stood along the railing. She took out her phone and showed him the photo of a large suitcase.

"What do you see?" she asked.

"A suitcase," he replied.

"Nope. This is my ticket out of here," she said.

Adonis turned to leave. She held him by the arm.

"Listen to me! I saw this crazy story from years ago about a girl who had her boyfriend kill her mom. Then they fit her into a big suitcase, just like this one, put it in a cab and then got it away. I can fit in one of these!"

"That's a very crazy story to use to prove your point. Don't you think it's a bit weird to use someone's unfortunate murder to justify a flawed escape plan? Are you listening to yourself?"

Chanel almost shouted back, then chose not to. She whispered, "I'm tired of this place. If you care about me, please get me out of here!"

"I remember you saying that I am not supposed to care about you. What's changed, huh?"

"Come on, Adonis—"

He held his hand up, "No. If you care about my job, you will not ask me again."

"I thought you were better than this," she said.

The words stung him, and he grit his teeth to keep himself in check.

"We don't need to talk, you know. See you around, Chanel,' he said, as he walked away, head held high.

He headed out of the office. He needed to clear his head. He called the cabbie who had driven him to Macaulay street. The driver was happy to come by, because their first ride together had given him a big payday.

"Where to?" the cab driver asked.

Adonis replied, "Um, 13 Coronation street."

"That's some way out, across the train tracks. You might come back a little late if it's a round trip," the cab driver said.

"Well, we can catch the sunset when there, right?"

"Not in that neighborhood. Security is not its strong point."

"I'll make it a fast one," Adonis reassured him.

The cab rolled down the street and disappeared in the traffic.

He soon saw why the cab driver was concerned. Coronation Street was on 'the other side of the tracks', a phrase that meant the poorer part of town. The homes were old two-storey blocks with peeling paint, asbestos roofs and rugged lawns. Streets were rougher than ideal, and there were groups of idle men around the corners. Music blared across many houses, possibly a tonic for the woes they faced daily. As they went past house number seven, they encountered a small group of kids happily playing hopscotch on the tarmac road.

"Here we are," the driver said, as they drove past the target house. Adonis spotted a man working a grill on the front lawn. The driver kept rolling for a few more feet then came to a stop.

Adonis wanted to take more time to study the man, but the driver was jittery.

"It's not safe here, so go talk to the man. Keep it quick. I'll turn the car around and wait," the driver said.

Adonis nodded and stepped out of the car. He walked fast towards the house, only slowing down as he neared its rickety gate.

He could see the old man's bald head popping above the fence as he drew closer, and when he came to a stop, he was finally able to see him well. The man wore a Hawaiian shirt that was unbuttoned to reveal a gray vest underneath. He had jean shorts and slip-ons, a true summer look. Reggae music filtered through from the open front door. The old man swayed to the music as he flipped pieces of meat patty.

"Hello, sir," Adonis said with a polite wave.

The man looked up with an intense stare. "What do you want?"

"Um, my name is Simon and—"

"I don't want to know your name. I asked you what you want?" the man said firmly.

Adonis hesitated, but the man was not in the mood to wait. He reached down to his right and lifted up a shotgun. His aim settled squarely on Adonis's chest.

"I'm going to ask you one more time, boy. What do you want?"

"Please, don't shoot me. I am here to ask you about Teddy Campbell."

"There's no Teddy Campbell here."

"I understand he went missing and—"

"I said he isn't here! Get your ass off my gate," the man ordered.

"Kindly sir, I—"

The man cocked the shotgun. "Are you deaf?"

"No, I'm not deaf," Adonis stuttered.

"Then run, boy. Run!" the man hissed.

Adonis was already sprinting towards the cab, almost tripping over himself in the process.

"Let's go, let's go, *let's go!*" he shouted at the driver. The cab had already started moving so Adonis clumsily jumped in. They accelerated past the house; the man's gun trained on them.

"I told you, this is not the place to look for sunsets!" the cab driver shouted as they raced away, narrowly dodging the now screaming group of kids.

CHAPTER EIGHT

ADONIS GOT HOME still shaking. He found his mother watching TV. Dmitri had already left, while his sisters were in their room. Ten minutes after he arrived, he was still sweating.

"It can't be that hot outside, Addie," his mother said.

"Let me hit the shower," he said, as he headed to his room.

When he got back to the living room in a fresh change of clothes, his mother was waiting.

"Are you okay Addie?" she asked.

"Yeah, I'm okay. Why?"

"You walked in here like you were being chased. Is something wrong?"

"Nothing's wrong, Ma. What's for dinner?"

"We are doing takeaway tonight," she replied. "I've already ordered the pizza."

"Just one?"

"Of course not!"

There was silence for a moment.

"So, you are not going to tell your mother what's wrong with you? I told you that after this Gail situation, I am not interested in secrets here," she said firmly.

"It's nothing, Ma, just work. There has been a lot of pressure. Plus, we have the new artistes getting their footing. It can get to you sometimes," he said.

"All right. If that's what you're going with, I won't argue. It's also been a long day looking after your sister, so a little peace right now is what we both need," she said.

"How is she?"

"She's getting her moods and strength back. Her appetite is still rubbish. She didn't eat a thing and when she did, she threw up. That is why we are doing pizza today. It is tiring to cook a whole buffet all day every day just to get her taste buds kicking," Bernice replied.

Adonis understood, and sometimes felt guilty that all the hard work to get Gail back on her feet was being done by everyone except him.

"Dmitri says she should be out of the woods soon," he reassured her.

"He's doing a good job, Dmitri. I did not know him that well, but over the last few days I can see why he is your friend. Very smart and reliable. But I told you, he will be gone soon. He has a life too," she replied.

"I hear you." Adonis knew that this was inevitable. However, it was never going to be long term anyway. The idea was for Dmitri to get her out of immediate danger, and then the family would take care of her to ensure she didn't relapse. They would have to work around the clock keeping an eye on her.

"Her teacher called me today, just to check in. I told her as soon as she is ready, she will be back. I just don't know what to say to her about being on the streets. I don't mind the idea of taking her to school and coming back, like the old days. But she's a grown girl. She needs to know how to navigate the negative bits. There are just too many influences out there," she said.

"It will be fine, Ma. Let me go and check on her."

Adonis found Gail and Marissa watching a movie on their shared laptop.

"Marissa, can I talk to Gail for a minute?"

"Sure," Marissa replied. She got up and left.

"Hey, Fireman," Gail said.

"Hey, Princess. How was your day?" he asked, sitting next to her on the bed.

"Decent. I didn't throw up today," she said, lifting up her hands as if she just won a race, "Isn't that awesome?"

"That's awesome. But you are not eating I'm told."

"Well, my tongue seems to be on holiday. But it will be back. Is the pizza here?"

"It's on its way. Still itchy?"

"No, thank God. Those messed me up for a bit. Dmitri was good helping me get over that. He's a cold turkey whisperer," she said.

Adonis laughed. "A cold turkey whisperer, huh?"

"Yep. He knocks it out of the park. I still get shakes though, but he tells me that they will go soon," she said with a dry laugh.

"You had us really worried there," he said.

"I know. I'm sorry," she replied.

"Where did you get the stuff?" he asked.

She went quiet then shook her head.

"Just some guy. I really do not want to talk about it because that's the past. I don't want to revisit the past; I only want to think about the future now."

"But sometimes what caused you to do this came from the past, and you need to work to avoid it."

"I will. Trust me I will," she replied.

"Do you wanna talk about why you did it?"

"Come on, Addie! We said future-talk only up in here, okay?" she protested.

"Okay, okay. I hear you. So, what does the future you are aiming for look like?"

"I want to clear school then get into university. I have to be there for you and Ma and Marissa. I have to be better," she said.

"You will, Princess. That's a sure thing," he said, as he hugged her.

"Thank you for not taking me to rehab," she said. "It would have broken me."

"I know," he said.

🌴

Marissa had walked in just as her mother was finishing a call.

"… you know, you can come just for one hour. Talk to her and then let me know if there's something I can do to help her—"

When Bernice noticed her daughter walking in, she quickly cut the call. "All right, I'll talk to you soon. Bye."

"Who is that?" Marissa asked.

"Just a friend of mine from church," her mother replied with a smile.

"I hope it's not for another prayer meeting, Ma."

"Prayer is important, Marissa. Do not play with it. Anyway, watch some TV," she said, throwing the remote towards her daughter.

As she watched the channels flip, she knew she would eventually have to tell them the truth. She just hoped they were going to take it well.

†

The following week, Adonis was at his station working when Gunner called.

"Where are you A.D.?"

"At my office. Why?"

"I need you to go and find Chanel," Gunner said.

"Wait, what happened?" He secretly hoped she had not run away.

"She's supposed to reshoot some scenes from the video, but she's acting up. Go and get her from the hotel room and bring her to the studio," he said.

"But why a reshoot? I thought the videos were just for internal training?"

"After the preview, the boss decided her track can actually be released as a single. When we do a single release, we do it properly. So, stop the questions and do what I tell you," he said.

Adonis sighed. "There's a small problem here."

"What problem?" Gunner asked.

"She won't talk to me. We had an argument last week and—"

Gunner cut him off, "I don't give a damn. Go and do your job." With that, he hung up.

"I'm sorry about the other day," Adonis said.

He did not believe a word of it, because she was actually at fault for that argument. But after standing outside her door for twenty minutes, this was a last-ditch effort to get her to open it.

It worked, because moments later the door flew open. She stood there wearing a tank top and booty shorts, with her hair tied in pigtails.

"Why do men apologize for things they are not wrong about?"

"Are you going to let me in or you going to make a scene in the hallway?" he asked.

She pondered for a moment then let him in. As she soon as she got to the center of the room, she continued her inquiry.

"Are you going to answer my question now?"

"Because women choose not to," he replied.

"Manipulation. That is the reason. That is what you are here to do," she said.

"If that's how you feel about it then why did you let me in?"

"To tell it to you directly," she replied.

"And?"

"And nothing," she replied.

He moved closer. "Why are you so hardheaded?

"I'm not," she replied.

"Prove it," he said.

She stepped forward until she pressed up against him, looking him in the eye. They could feel the electricity drawing them together again. Instinctively their lips hovered over each other before connecting, soft and slow.

She wrapped her arms around him. Lips still locked, they moved toward the bed, easing themselves into it. He traced his lips onto her neck and down towards her breasts as she arched towards him. They took off their clothes one by one, slow and intentional. As their bodies engulfed each other, they savored every slow kiss, every rub, and every stroke.

Ten minutes later, they cuddled on the bed.

"I've got your back," he said.

"Are you talking about right now or figuratively?" she asked jokingly.

"Both," he said, squeezing her a little more, "I'll look after you. No matter what."

For the first time in days, Chanel smiled with genuine happiness.

🌴

Adonis and Chanel went back to the studio. She was in high spirits, but they had agreed she could not be too elated lest they were viewed with suspicion. So, she maintained a mellow attitude, which was a relief for Adonis because Gunner was there. She no longer had qualms about wearing the new outfit; she had changed into a fitted miniskirt and bustier, which is what they needed for the scene. When the video shoot began Gunner left, satisfied that things were finally in motion. Adonis chose to hang around just to make sure there were no more fireworks between Chanel and the crew.

Half an hour into the shoot, the receptionist tapped Adonis's shoulder. "Vernon wants to see you," she said.

When he got the office, he found Vernon and Gunner waiting for him. Vernon sat behind his desk. Gunner stood next to him.

"How's it going?" Vernon asked.

"It's good, sir," Adonis replied.

"I hear you have been doing quite a bit of conflict management with the artists," Vernon said. Adonis cast a glance at Gunner, whose face remained expressionless.

"Just a bit. Nothing fancy. To help them manage the situation," Adonis said.

Vernon stood up and went around the desk, and then perched himself at the front of it.

"What's the situation, Adonis?" Vernon asked.

Adonis was not sure whether it was a trick question or not, so he played it as straight as he could.

"The intense schedule. Getting to grips with life as a performer," Adonis replied.

Vernon nodded as he looked right into Adonis's eyes.

"You know about my father?" Vernon asked.

"I have heard about him. He was one of the leading real estate managers in the islands," Adonis replied.

"In the islands. That is what I was looking for. It tells me you can see the big picture. So, I got a short story. When I was a teenager, around sixteen I think, I stole my father's bike. Not a bicycle. A two-stroke dirt bike. Why did I steal it? My dad used to take us to the motocross park with my mom, and we would watch him racing. It was astounding how fast these guys could go, jumping over little hills and dodging each other around the track. Kicking up all sorts of dirt. They used to do it for bets as well, not just trophies. My dad liked betting on people's bikes, especially if it was a bike he liked. He would win most of those races, he was simply too good. So, because of his betting wins, he ended up having around ten amazing dirt bikes that he won from other racers filling up our garage. As I got older, I just wanted to try it out. So, I stole one and rode it near the beach close to home. I tore the hell out of that thing! It was good fun."

Vernon paused here to study his gold-plated ring.

"When I went back home, I visualized boasting to my father that I was finally going to be as good a rider as he was. But when I got there, I found the police. My dad had reported it stolen and they were getting a statement from him. So, imagine the sight of his own son riding in with the stolen bike. I can laugh at it now, but back then it was a bit embarrassing. He gave me a good beating after that, and the ten bikes were moved to a warehouse the next day. I never did become as good a rider as he was, just because of one evening of teenage ambition."

Vernon's gaze went back to Adonis.

"Chanel is the most talented artist we have ever signed. Oceania, God rest her soul, is our biggest right now, but Chanel has everything. I think you know what I mean, right?" Vernon asked.

Adonis nodded.

"Good. My advice to you is this: look after her if you know what is good for you. Don't steal the bike and head to the beach, like me," Vernon said with a smile.

"I'll do what you need me to do, sir," Adonis replied.

"That's what I like to hear. You can go," Vernon said.

Adonis left the room. Vernon kept playing with the ring on his finger.

"He's banging her, isn't he?"

"Possibly," Gunner replied.

"Let's hope he doesn't get her pregnant," Vernon replied. "Are the VR kits ready?"

"They are being shipped in as we speak."

Vernon grunted his approval. He stood up and straightened his suit. He picked up a folder from his desk and tossed it at Gunner, who caught it just in time.

"What's this?" Gunner asked.

"Read it. Some startup company called Key-Tech is making waves in the digital space. They have an interesting product that helps users get music at lower rates. They've been at it for a year, but it seems to be catching on faster than expected."

"What do you want to do about it?"

"Find out who runs it, and their tech. I want to know what their play is, because we are going to cut their market share."

"I'll get to it," Gunner said, as he walked to the door.

"Don't be afraid to get your hands dirty," Vernon instructed.

"When I was a kid, I liked playing with dirt. Nothing has changed," Gunner replied.

CHAPTER NINE

THE NEXT DAY, six hundred VR kits packed in highly padded boxes arrived at the Sephtis entertainment offices. The place was buzzing with excitement. Vernon made four of them available for the staff to try out. It was part of selling the dream to them. Each VR headset had a gold-plated lining, with a small Sephtis logo strategically placed. Customized wireless headphones were also part of the deal, giving noise-cancelling premium sound to the wearer.

To appease them, Vernon and Gunner let the artistes experience them first.

"This will be you in two months. Get familiar with it," Vernon said.

Adonis and Chanel cast quick glances at each other, careful to make their interaction look as casual as possible. Each artist experienced a five-minute VR concert by Oceania. By the time their turn was over, they were waving their hands in the air, cheering, clapping, or dancing. The gear left a positive impression on all the artistes, including Chanel.

Adonis wanted to give it a go, too. Luckily, he and Leroy, being at the forefront of digital strategy, were next in line. As he put on the kit, he had no idea what to expect. He had used VR gear on video games at home, but it's always a different experience with any new visual medium. He also needed to experience an Oceania performance one more time.

The visuals he was watching took him back to one of the performances they did on the road at the Switch Arena, one of the biggest stages they attended. He could hear the cheering crowd, and then Oceania appeared. She came down on a reinforced cable from the ceiling, surrounded by smoke. Her silhouette, shapely as ever, walked into the light and she began singing her track, "Rock the Night." As she performed, the crowd's cheering got louder. The sound, crisp, clear and rich filled Adonis's consciousness and he was lost in the moment. He danced and cheered and danced some more. By the time her song ended, he was hot and sweaty.

He put down the headset and wiped tears off his eyes. He smiled.

"That was so dope, so dope," Adonis said, slowly clapping. Gunner watched him. He could tell under the layer of happiness was some sadness for Adonis.

Leroy shook his head in disbelief. "I'm going to ask them to give us one of these bad boys," he said to Adonis.

"You are getting two actually," Gunner said. Leroy punched his fists in the air.

As Adonis walked to the FXX office, he was a mixed bag of raw emotion, still awash with the images of Oceania. He owed her justice. When lunch hour came, he left the office looking for it. He phoned the cab driver.

"I'm not going back there again," the driver said.

"It's lunch time, it's not as dangerous," Adonis said.

"No, the guy you went to see is dangerous. Nope, not for this ride. Sorry," the driver replied.

Adonis walked down the street and found another cab driver asleep in his car.

"Can you take me to Coronation Street?"

"Sure. Twelve dollars one way," he said.

What? It's a twenty-dollar return ride," Adonis protest.

"Thirty dollars and I will take you and return you," the driver said.

Adonis gave it another thought. He was blowing his budget.

"All right," Adonis agreed.

As they crossed the train tracks, he realized he had taken no precautions. He was just operating on his emotional drive, which was foolish. What would he say to the gun-toting man?

They arrived at the house, and Adonis instructed the driver to turn around, and park two spots away from the house just in case.

"Keep the engine running," Adonis said.

"I always do in these parts," the driver replied. "Just don't stay too long."

Adonis used the only cautionary tactic he had left now: he watched the home first for a few minutes, waiting. The grill was not outside, and the man was not in sight. Should he go and knock? That may be the only way to settle it, because each minute they spent on the street made them easy targets. He also kept an eye out for any strange characters watching him. There were some at the far end of the street. After a few minutes, he could not wait any longer. He got out and walked briskly towards the house. His eyes kept darting around, ready to react at the slightest movement.

Just as he was about to get into the gate, the front door opened. He braced himself. A woman in her thirties emerged, alone. He watched her for a few seconds. The man did not appear. She was hanging laundry on a short line to one side of the house. He made his move, walking up to her.

"Sorry to bother you," he began, "Is this Teddy Campbell's home?"

She turned around to him. "Yes, it is. Who's asking?"

"My name is Simon. I'm doing a feature about his music career and wonder if you could tell me something about him," he said, taking out a notebook and pen. This time, he wanted to look the part.

She paused briefly. "A feature for where?"

"*Entertainment Weekly.* It's a new publication. We want to trace the history of musicians, especially those we lost while they were in their prime. Where can I find him?" he replied.

"At the cemetery," she replied. "He can't speak for himself though."

He was shaken. He was not going to get used to the news of someone's death.

"I'm sorry for your loss. When did he die?"

"Two years ago. They said it was an accidental overdose," she replied.

"That was after he retired?"

"Retired? That's what his publicist wanted us to say. He died before all that talk," she replied.

"Do you remember where he died, and the name of his publicist?"

"They found him in the Remus Hotel lying on the floor. She worked for that recording company, can only remember the name Renée," she said.

"Thank you." He would have asked her if he could come back but he did not really think it would be wise, especially if the man learned that he had been talking to her.

He walked back to the car.

"Where to now?" the driver asked.

"Blue Lake," Adonis replied. He needed to talk to Dmitri.

⁂

"I have to admit, I am beginning to think that you have something here," Dmitri said.

Adonis nodded. He had not touched his coffee, while Dmitri was halfway through his.

"I'm just wondering what this means," Adonis said.

"You know what it means," Dmitri said.

"I don't think that it's a good thing to keep digging. If Gunner is anything to go by, these are violent people," Adonis said.

"Are you willing to walk away? It is an option. The only problem is if it happens again…"

"I won't be able to live with it."

"So, what's next?" Dmitri asked.

"I can only prove my theory by checking the album sales. To get to the actual records in the FFX system, I need clearance. Only Leroy, Vernon, and Gunner have it."

"But you now have a good working relationship with Leroy," Dmitri said.

"Yeah, but this is high level security stuff. He will not give that to me without suspicion or losing his job if Vernon found out. We'll have to find another way."

"We?" Dmitri asked.

"You're going to help me. I can't do this alone," Adonis said.

Dmitri sighed. He knew there was no getting out of this.

Adonis continued, "If both artists hit their peak just before they died, then—"

"Then it would mean your theory is correct," Dmitri said. "Sephtis kills them and then makes millions from their deaths."

"No one has died there in over a year," Adonis said, "so maybe you're right. People die every day."

"Except Oceania. And if they are back to it, then the next target could come from the new artists they've just signed. Chanel—"

"Nah, let's not talk about it anymore," Adonis said.

It was a little too dark to think about it. He knew what he *had* to do.

⊤

Terek Thomas was a tall lanky man, with long dreadlocks that fell over his shoulders. His hair had long developed gray streaks, which had spread to his long beard too. He tried to keep them as fresh as possible while on the road. His face was always a smiling one, because life was too short and too hard to be grim-faced. He wore a black shirt with green leaf patterns, a sleeveless leather jacket, a pair of scruffy jeans, and his trademark brown leather boots. On his back was his long acoustic guitar in its pack and on his side was a small travel bag. He loved travelling light and did not mind wearing the same clothes for several days at a time.

He believed in staying frugal and in the moment. Mother Nature would always look after you. If she cared about the birds, why would you worry about yourself?

He looked up at the streetlamps above him and wished they were stars. He was an unabashed stargazer. He constantly searched for constellations in the night sky when he was on the road. He carried a star map and a portable telescope, which he used every night he had a clear dark sky. He picked up the habit when he had to quit the bars and the alcohol and could not sleep at night. In some ways, you could say he had been looking for his own North star, something that would add a flavor of meaning to his life. Although he loved the roadshows and the audience reactions was always a high, he had never filled in the hole that was his purpose. He was one of the most sought-after guitarists in the islands. All the big bands had worked with him, and whenever there was a festival or major concert he had to be there. Yet, when alone in the room after all the fanfare was done, he did not recognize himself, nor his purpose in the world.

The lack of purpose was one reason why he could not stand the thought of building a family. What kind of direction could he give if he didn't know where he was going? Of course, his heavy drinking had not helped his marriage with Bernice, so when she threatened to throw him out about it, he beat her to it. He simply woke up, left, and never looked back. She was more realistic, grounded, and a safe pair of hands.

He kept in touch through phone calls and the occasional video call, but that was it. He usually wondered how fast the money he earned always ran out before he could send any to Bernice.

As he headed to Bernice's house, the home he had walked away from all those years ago, it had changed. The roads were smoother, and the sidewalk well paved. Finally, there were streetlamps. When he left, they were not there. They were not starry, but they made him smile.

He was close to Bernice's house when he noticed some movement coming from the side window. It was in the shadows, but he could clearly make out the figure of a person. The figure jumped out from the window, which was not high off the ground. The window slowly and quietly closed. The figure, a young girl, straightened out her pants and slunk away from the house, staying in the shadows. Terek slowed down, pacing himself to see where she would go. Moments later, she emerged from a side street to his left, passing him as if he was not there. She was young, possibly sixteen. For a moment he thought of going after her, to find out what she was doing. Then he thought against it.

He noticed that the streetlamp right outside Bernice's house had started flickering, just like she had told him. He smiled. He walked up to the front door and rang the bell.

Adonis was not amused when he heard the doorbell ring so many times late at night. He woke up and found his mother already at the door. What he saw enraged him: she was in a deep embrace with his father, Terek.

Welcome back," she said.

"Thank you, sweetheart," Terek replied.

"How was the trip?"

"Nothing crazy. You know I'm built for the road," Terek replied. This reply stung Bernice, but she hid it well behind her smile.

"Well, we are going to have to change that sometime," she said.

"I'm open to suggestions, "Terek replied, ever the charmer.

Gail and Marissa were over the moon, running and hugging Terek. They did not believe their eyes, and neither could Adonis. He looked at his mother, and she was smiling with fullness. He understood that she wanted the family to be back together again, but he hated the disappointment his father continually wrought on her.

"You are both so beautiful," Terek said to his daughters.

When Terek approached Adonis, his son was not interested in the proffered hand. Terek withdrew it.

"Hello, son."

"Hi, Terek," Adonis replied.

"You look well."

"It's the product of good energy," Adonis replied.

"Your mother tells me you got a new job," Terek said.

"Yeah. It is pretty good. Ma, can you tell him more about it on my behalf? I have a phone call to make," Adonis said, taking out his phone.

"Addie, please," Bernice told her son, but Adonis was already walking out the front door.

Outside, he took in a deep breath. He needed to calm down the rage that filled his chest. It was not working.

Why was his father back here? What was he trying to achieve with this?

He simply could not stand the presence of the man. He

knew Terek was going to walk out on them as soon as he could get the chance, probably with some family savings. Why didn't his mother see through his lie?

He had to be patient, for the sake of his mother. He looked at his phone again. There was still someone else he could tell the truth. He dialed.

It rang several times. "Hello," a feeble, female voice said.

"Hey, Chanel. Did I wake you?" he asked, stating the obvious.

"It's a little late, so what do you think?" she replied.

"I know I did. Listen, there's something you need to know."

"I'm half asleep. Can't it wait till morning?"

"That's up to you. Do you want to live or die when you wake up tomorrow?" he asked gravely.

"I actually don't mind dying in the morning," Chanel said, and hung up on him.

CHAPTER TEN

ADONIS FUMED. SHE wasn't going to take him seriously unless he had some evidence. He let the night chill hit him. An hour later, he was calm enough to get back into the house, heading straight to his room.

The next morning Adonis and Dmitri met at the street café for an early breakfast. Adonis wasn't keen on having a big family breakfast with Terek in the picture. He also needed his best friend's advice before heading to the office.

"Listen, you need to help me crack into the office's A.I. program," Adonis said.

"You said it's the latest Haze system, right? I told you I can't do that remotely," Dmitri replied, biting into a conch fritter.

"What do you mean? It's just a computer. It can be hacked."

"Do you know why they are using limited issue Genesys

computers? Because they only want them to be accessed by a limited number of people. Those things are tanks in our tech world. You can only get in when sitting in front of one."

"And if I say I can get in front of it, I can then install a backdoor that can be accessed remotely?" Adonis asked.

"It should be possible," Dmitri replied.

"There's nothing you got that I could use, some malware from some hacker or something?"

Dmitri laughed and shook his head.

"Come on. Could Kai know something?" Adonis pressed.

"Maybe. I have to ask him though. Why haven't you tried in the Crab's Nest community?"

"You said I should avoid giving too much detail there. I need one person on this, not a whole bunch of people from the dark web."

"I hear you. All right, let me see what I can do," Dmitri replied. "But, why don't you try asking Leroy for the password?"

"I told you that won't work. I'll have to do something special to get it off him."

"Special like what?" Dmitri asked. Adonis held Dmitri's gaze for a few seconds.

"You feel me?" Adonis asked.

"Here's what you should do," Dmitri started, leaning in to whisper secrets we cannot hear.

↑

On his way to work, Adonis passed by a nutrition center and bought a small jar of whey protein powder. Dmitri had elaborated a few crazy ideas, which didn't work, but this one might.

When they used to go to the gym together, they would drink protein shakes made from whey protein. This always made them run to the toilets fifteen minutes later because it induced bowel discomfort. Since it was based on a shared experience, they both agreed it was best suited to give Leroy a stomach upset. Half an hour would be all Adonis needed to access the files on Leroy's computer.

At the office, he checked in on Leroy, and offered to make him a cup of coffee. He made the coffee a little stronger than usual and added just a little milk. He was about to add a scoop of the whey powder but then stopped. He was jittery. What if Leroy could taste it and noticed something was off? Adonis stopped. *Maybe tomorrow*, he resolved. He took the steaming coffee to Leroy, and then headed to a meeting to strategize the new artists' album launches. Gunner was leading the meeting.

"So as your contracts clearly state, you will receive training from a dance choreographer as well as a stage presence coach as you prepare for your album launches. We expect you to produce the goods. Any questions?" Gunner asked, looking around the boardroom, his gaze lingering a little longer on Randy Rah. No one had an objection.

"Great! We start tomorrow," Gunner said, as he waved them off.

As they walked out of the meeting towards the cafeteria, Adonis went up to Chanel. "So, how are you feeling about tomorrow?"

"You know what? I'm actually looking forward to it. I really want to see how it goes," Chanel replied cheerily.

"Someone's become optimistic lately," Adonis mused.

"Well, I realized sometimes growth can stretch your

seams, more than you are used to. So, I am now looking at it as growth. I like a good challenge," she replied.

Adonis shook his head, unconvinced.

Chanel grabbed his arm. "Come, let's take one of the cubicles," she said.

"Chanel, we said that we're not supposed to give the office ideas about us," he whispered, as he tried to wrestle his arm away. She wouldn't let go.

"To hell with that! You are going to sit with me, and no one is going to do anything about it," she replied.

Not wanting to draw attention, he went along. They secured a cubicle that overlooked the car park and street below.

"That thing I said about growth. That's a bunch of BS I was trying to feed you. I can tell it didn't land," she said.

"Not one bit," he confessed.

Chanel took a deep breath and looked outside as she spoke. "When I was a toddler, my parents were pretty rich. Then there was big hurricane that tore up my neighborhood, and my family has not had it easy since. I had to fight with my parents for an education, because whenever you have fee arrears all they want to do is kick you out. It made me hardheaded. Pushing through when the odds are against you," she laughed, and then went on, "because if I had given up on school, I would be kicking myself out of an education. I couldn't let that happen, no matter how uncomfortable it made me."

"Same principle here?"

"Exactly. I have to make it here. My parents deserve a good life and I plan to give it back to them."

"You're not afraid of losing yourself in the chaos?" he asked.

She laughed again. "I love chaos. You know that by now, right?" she said, as her hand reached for his and rubbed it affectionately. He wanted to pull it back, but for some reason didn't.

"You're getting dangerously bold."

"Just illustrating that I love chaos. With actions," she said teasingly, pulling her hand away.

"So… there's nothing that Sephtis can do that would be a deal breaker for you, right?" he asked.

Chanel thought for one second and shook her head. "Nope, nothing. I think I have a good idea of what they want, and I think I can handle it. Besides, I signed a contract for ten years."

Adonis shook his head. "Wait, what? A ten-year contract? How many albums are we talking about?"

"Five albums spaced out. If I record fast enough, I don't have to hang around that long."

"But that's—"

"Slavery? A factory? Yeah, I told you it was," she said, "but I have made peace with it. I suggest you do the same," she said to his shocked face.

Their cappuccinos arrived. She took her steaming mug and raised it.

"Let's toast to success and good money in the years ahead!" she said smiling.

He reluctantly raised his mug to meet hers.

🌴

But I'm still there grinin' and winnin'
just like the next foldin' paper
Thinkin' of ways to load another caper
It's a cold twist to know that I can slang all night
And slang all day but never have the courage to pray.

The Richie Rich rap lyrics filtered to Gunner's ears as he sat in his car waiting. He had parked under the shade in a side street near the central business district. He was watching the people walking in the street.

A man wearing a leather jacket walked by his car and entered it, sitting in the back-left passenger seat. Gunner turned off the music.

"You're late," Gunner said.

"I had to get away without raising eyebrows," the man replied.

"So, what do you have for me?" Gunner asked.

"It's all in here," the man said, handing Gunner a small chip the size of a peanut.

"How much data?"

"Two terabytes. It will show you quite a bit about the infrastructure they have built. But you will not be able to access the architecture of the ATS program."

"Why not? I thought that's one of your deliverables?"

"They have layered security that I couldn't figure out. Someone who knows what they're doing might be able to get in. But I doubt it."

"They're using block chain, aren't they?"

"Yes, they are. Just like you," the man replied.

Gunner grunted. He didn't like the news, but it was progress nevertheless.

He reached into the glove compartment next to him and took out a thick, brown package. He handed it to the man.

"There's your cash. Note that because you haven't given me access to the program you still owe me. I collect all my debts," Gunner said.

"Understood."

"Is there anything else you want to tell me?"

"Key-Tech is going to get the exclusive rights to distribute in the region."

"What are you talking about?"

"They are negotiating with the governor to get monopoly access rights for the ATS. In future, if you want to use the system, you have to go through them. They will have all entertainment companies by the balls," the man explained.

Gunner's eyes narrowed. "Is that so? How far are they with that?"

"Still in the early stages. They recently sent their initial proposal to the governor for review. It would normally take a few months. But I know they're paying good money for it, so I expect it to be approved in the next two weeks."

"Good. Keep me posted on how that is going."

"Sure."

The man pocketed the envelope, then stepped out of the car and disappeared into the city crowd. Gunner tapped the steering wheel, cursing under his breath. They had been trying to get the same deal with the governor but had gotten the cold shoulder. Now he understood why.

Something needed to be done. Fast.

🌴

'I have to make it.'

Chanel's words kept ringing in Adonis's head as he left the office. They reminded him of Oceania. He felt a strong urge to go and talk to her parents and find out how they were doing. To let them know that their daughter was an amazing performer who inspired him. To let them know that he had connected with her as a person.

He found himself outside Oceania's home. It was an hour's ride by bus during rush hour. He stood outside for a few minutes, wondering what he would say. Then knocked the door and waited.

"They're not around," a voice said. He turned to his right and saw a young woman, their neighbor, staring at him.

"Sorry, I was just checking on them."

"Well, they are not here. Who are you?"

"I knew their daughter who passed on."

"Do you want to leave a message?"

"No need, I will come by another time," Adonis replied. He left quickly.

When he got home, Adonis was not in the best mood. Two things had deflated him. He didn't manage to get the password from Leroy, and he had not shared his condolences with Oceania's family.

He tried to delay getting home so that he would arrive after dinnertime. His mother always served dinner at seven in the evening. It was nine o'clock when he stepped onto the front porch. However, he had not counted on one delaying factor: Terek. So, when Adonis walked in and found them in the middle of dinner, his heart sank.

"Come join us!" his mother Bernice said. The table was laid as if a house party was going on. There was a good amount of chicken and steak, fried rice, pasta, vegetable salad, and roasted potatoes, all topped off with a rich serving of gravy and groundnut sauce. Terek, who was licking his lips as he wolfed down his meal, waved him over.

"Come on over, son. Plenty of food for everyone. I suspect your mother is here to fatten us for some reason," he teased. Bernice poked his forearm and laughed.

Adonis reluctantly sat at the table. He served himself some chicken and potatoes with groundnut sauce.

"So, how was your day?" Bernice asked.

There was a pregnant pause as everyone waited for him to talk.

"It was good, but tiring," Adonis replied.

"Working hard?" Terek asked.

Adonis didn't reply. Another awkward pause.

"He's one of the most hardworking people I know," Gail said to break the silence.

"How are you feeling today?" Adonis asked her.

"I'm great! Even Dmitri didn't stay long today," she replied.

"Why not?" he asked.

"Dad said that he will help me out from now on," Gail said.

"He did, huh?" Adonis asked.

"Yeah. You know I have a history... I mean, an understanding of addiction. And I beat it," Terek said.

Adonis shook his head as he bit into a piece of chicken.

"Why are you shaking your head?" Terek asked.

Adonis didn't reply, simply shrugging.

"Boy, if you have something to say you better say it," Terek warned.

Adonis smiled to himself. He put down his utensils, pulled back the chair and stood up.

"Thanks, Ma, for the food. I'm full," he declared.

"Addie, get serious. You have barely touched what you served."

Adonis picked the plate of food. "I'll finish off the rest in my room, I can't take another second looking at this piece of shit," he replied.

With that, he headed to his bedroom. As he walked away, he could hear murmurs behind him. He thought Terek would shout at him, but it didn't come. Maybe Bernice held him back. Adonis didn't care. He was not going to make a stranger who called himself his father get comfortable. This was not his home, and Adonis was determined to make him know it.

CHAPTER ELEVEN

ADONIS WAS UP before sunrise, earlier than his usual time. He had received a text from Dmitri to meet him at the café early. He freshened up and was keen to leave before anyone was up. As he walked quietly to the front door, a pleasant aroma came to him. There was a light in the kitchen. Curious, he walked to it and found his mother Bernice cooling a batch of chocolate chip cookies.

"Good morning, Ma," he said.

"You're up early," she replied.

"Yeah. I have to get to work. Got a lot on my plate today."

"You know what else you need on your plate?" she asked. She picked up a cookie and held it up to him.

Chocolate chip cookies were his favorite.

"I wouldn't mind starting my day with some of that,"

Adonis said. Bernice smiled, and quickly stacked some cookies into a plastic lunchbox.

As she handed it to him, she said, "Someday you will need to talk to him instead of avoiding him."

Adonis took the lunchbox. "That day is not today. Have a good one, Ma," he replied, kissing her forehead.

At the street café, he had to wait for ten minutes before Dmitri finally appeared.

"You are not having anything today?" Dmitri asked.

"Nah, I have my breakfast sorted. What's up?"

"Kai got me your gift," Dmitri replied. He took out a small box. Opening it, it had a chip inside. "Plug this into the chip port, that's all you have to do."

"What's in it?"

"A rootkit that will give us access to the system remotely. As soon as you do it, I will take it from there."

Adonis smiled. He put it in his pocket. "How much do I owe?"

"He's my brother, so it's on the house," Dmitri said.

As soon as he got to the office, Adonis ate the cookies with a mug of white coffee. As usual, his mother had made them rich with love. He was hardly halfway through the box and he was already full. He left the box on his desk and went to the studio on the next floor. He found the new artists rehearsing their choreography for their album launches. Unsurprisingly, Chanel was standing out, but so was Bruce. Led by a choreographer hired by Sephtis, they were shown the looks, the moves, and the set-ups they would each need to make their acts stand out.

Soon, each artist was having a good run as they grew in confidence. Watching Chanel work, Adonis could see that she would break records as the one natural performer. This reminded him about the password. He had to get it.

When he got back to his office, Leroy had arrived.

"Good morning Leroy,"

"Hey are those chocolate chip cookies?" Leroy asked.

"Yeah, they are."

"Awesome, can I have some? I was running late so I didn't get to take a bite."

"Yeah of course. You want a coffee with that?" Adonis asked. Leroy nodded.

Adonis headed to the kitchen and made him coffee. He then added some of the whey powder.

As soon as he got back, he realized he shouldn't have bothered.

He found Leroy retching while prostrate on the floor.

"Leroy! What's wrong?"

"Call… an …ambulance…nut allergy," Leroy managed to gasp.

Adonis could not believe it. A nut allergy? He called for an ambulance, hoping it didn't get out of hand. He didn't have to wait long. The paramedics were there in five minutes. By then, other co-workers had come to help, but Leroy was still in a bad state.

As he was wheeled out, Adonis went to his side.

"Leroy, I'll handle things. What's your password?"

Leroy waved his hand away.

"Come on Leroy. Let me take care of things."

Leroy started whispering. Adonis realized Leroy wouldn't voice it loudly for everyone to hear. He moved closer to Leroy and listened carefully. Five seconds later he stepped back and watched his boss get rolled away fast.

Vernon came to the door.

"What happened here?"

"Leroy ate some of my cookies. I didn't know he has a nut allergy."

"Damn! They hit him hard. He's stupid for not telling you that."

Adonis watched Vernon grimace.

"You can hold fort while he gets treatment?"

"I believe so. sir," Adonis replied.

"You better. It might be a day or two before he's back," Vernon said, and walked away.

↑

Twenty minutes after Leroy was rushed to hospital, Adonis sat in front of his computer. He managed to key in the password Leroy had given him, and he was immediately in the system proper.

Before him in all their glory were the year-by-year sales breakdowns for all the artists signed under Sephtis companies. They even had weekly analyses. The AI was able to track all global sales in real time, and this was possible because all the sales made were digital. The program was also able to gauge, through matching the artist's profile with the preferences of individual clients, and the marketability of an artist's brand. He started trawling, searching each artist's album launches and the sales that followed. Every artist had high sales after their launches, which was an indication of a good sales strategy by the company.

He then narrowed down to the sales of his persons of interest: Oceania, Teddy, and Flava. They hit the highest sales numbers of all the artistes on the roster after their album launches, with Oceania leading the numbers. Then he saw it. Once an artist hit ten million sales, combined with a marketability score of nine-out-of-ten, they soon died. It happened to Flava, to Teddy, and to Oceania.

The more he thought about it the more he was sure of it. Ten million sales and a nine-out-of-ten marketability score was the benchmark.

It was the kill switch.

He then checked the sales numbers after they died. All the numbers doubled, except for Oceania's, which was expected to triple in sales. With the new tech offerings they were giving, her margins would definitely be higher than the rest. He opened Chanel's sales numbers and saw that they were rising steadily. She was already at one million digital sales for her single and it was only the second day since its release. Her marketability score was at five and rising, as the AI collected data about news mentions and social media trends. The algorithm projected she would hit the ten million mark during or after her album launch and tour. He sighed.

He reached into his pocket, took out the chip Dmitri had given him and plugged it into the chip port. The chip immediately started copying a file into the system. It copied in five minutes. Adonis called Dmitri.

"It's done. Check on your end."

"All right."

Adonis waited for a minute.

"Yeah, I'm in," Dmitri said.

"What can you see?"

"Everything. Wow, this is a lot of stuff."

"Yeah, it is. And you're sure they can't track you?"

"Kai says the only way I can be tracked is if someone very good is able to find the hidden program. We are good."

"Check out the numbers. I can already see patterns, but I want you to tell me what you see. Oh, and for Chanel's sales, limit the numbers to eight million," Adonis instructed.

"Sure thing. Talk later."

🌴

When Gunner asked the Key-Tech management to meet him at the abandoned warehouse, he wasn't surprised when they refused. Arnold Key was an ambitious man but not a stupid one. However, meeting one of his rivals was not something he was going to shy away from especially if there was big money to be made. That was Gunner's sales pitch: a proposition that would ensure both companies remained in business and made good money out of a one-time deal. They agreed to meet at the Key-Tech offices at eight in the evening when the staff had gone home for the day.

When they arrived in two dark SUVs, Gunner and his men made an impression. He had an entourage of six men as they walked towards Arnold and his men, who were standing in front of his three-storey office building. Gunner had come as the only representative of his management, with five henchmen in tow. Vernon had wanted to come but Gunner insisted he would handle it alone.

"Are you Gunner?" Arnold asked, shaking his hand.

"Yes, it is. Mr. Arnold Key?" Gunner asked.

"The one and only," Arnold replied with a smile.

"Thank you for having us," Gunner said.

"Let's go in and talk business."

When they settled in the Key-Tech boardroom, Gunner and Arnold faced each other with their men flanking them.

"You told me that you have a proposition for me," Arnold began.

"Walls have ears sometimes. Are we okay here?"

"It's that kind of thing?"

"Yes, it's that kind of thing," Gunner replied.

"Then you have nothing to worry about."

"Let my men confirm that, kindly," Gunner said courteously.

One of Gunner's men moved around with a scanner, checking out the walls and furniture for any listening devices.

"I'll also need you to hand over your phones and have them taken out of the room," Gunner said.

"That's not necessary," Arnold said.

"It's for all our sakes," Gunner insisted.

One of Gunner's men moved around with a tray and they placed their phones in it. He then took the tray out of the room.

"Sorry for the inconvenience. Now we can talk," Gunner said with a smile, "What do you know about Advanced Social Targeting?"

Arnold cleared his throat. "I have heard of it. Why?"

Gunner was trying to trip him, and it was working. He knew Arnold had not only heard of it; he also knew Key-Tech was about to complete their AST system. The one the governor wanted instead of taking Sephtis's deal. An advanced artificial intelligence system, it would give any company an edge in target marketing.

"We have a system like that ready to roll out. But we wanted to target two different parts of the market," Gunner explained.

"You can still do that," Arnold said.

"No, we cannot, because we do not have a monopoly access license."

Arnold smiled. He realized Gunner knew about their secret meetings with the governor.

"You know about our ATS license already. Interesting," Arnold turned to look at his men, wondering who had snitched.

"We heard about it through the grapevine," Gunner replied, "And since you are about to receive it, we thought that it might be wise to make money from our primary market and then lease the rights to you for a secondary and tertiary market. We would then get a cut from the sales."

"How much are we talking about?" Arnold asked.

"Twenty percent from every sale."

"I think seven percent would be a better place for us to start talking, considering we will have the main license," Arnold replied.

Gunner twitched. The counteroffer was an insult. "Hmm. Seven per cent would be—"

The ringing of a phone cut him off. It rung for two seconds, but those two seconds had Key-Tech's men tense up.

"I thought we agreed no phones?" Arnold asked.

Gunner reached into his trouser pocket. As he did this, two Key-Tech men reached to their sides. Gunner now knew two of Arnold's men were armed.

"Sorry. I forgot," Gunner said, as he checked his phone. It was a text that read: *'A.D. went to Oceania's house.'* Gunner grunted.

"What are you doing with a phone?" Arnold asked again.

"Relax guys, it's not a big deal," Gunner said.

A shot rang out from the gun of one of Gunner's henchmen. The target, one of Arnold's men brandishing a gun, was hit in the chest and collapsed in his seat. Everyone started ducking as gunshots rang out. Gunner took out his Magnum pistol as he braced himself under the table.

One of Gunner's men was there to shield him as they backed away towards the door, but Gunner wasn't up for it. He pushed him away and started taking out the Key-Tech men. There were three left including Arnold, trying to get to the backdoor exit that led to another office. Gunner shot two while one of his men hit another. Arnold got shot in his leg and fell to the ground writhing in pain.

"Hold fire!" he ordered his men. He walked up to Arnold and saw him reaching for his bodyguard's gun.

"No, don't do that," Gunner warned.

Arnold stopped and grimaced in pain.

"Look, we can talk this out," Arnold pleaded.

"How much had you offered the governor?"

"What do you mean?"

"How much had you paid him and how much cut was he going to get from the deal?"

Arnold hesitated. Gunner pointed his Magnum at him.

"We gave him twenty million upfront. He would get twelve percent of sales," Arnold blurted out.

"And you were offering us seven per cent? *Seven?* That's what I call disrespect," Gunner said. He pulled the trigger, hitting Arnold twice in the chest. Arnold stopped moving, a pool of blood forming on the fresh carpet.

Gunner walked towards the door, telling his men to roll out. One had a bullet in his arm but was handling it.

"Wipe the footage on the security systems. Light up this place," Gunner ordered.

Two of his other men took out lighters and started filling up the trashcans with any paper they could find. One headed for the office kitchen and turned on the gas tap.

In a space of ten minutes, Gunner and his men cleared up all the security footage of their arrival at the office and took out the security guards as well. As the SUVs drove out, Gunner looked up and could see the office going up in flames. Sirens were already sounding in the distance.

Gunner turned to one of his men. "Reggie, I want you to take one of the cars and go stake out a guy called Adonis. He's one of my employees. I'll give you his number, picture, and address. I want to know everything he's doing, from the food he's eating to the women he's seeing. Everything."

CHAPTER TWELVE

ADONIS PLAYED WITH Chanel's hair as they lay in bed watching the widescreen television. It was playing *Machine Matchmaker*, a reality show about singles finding someone to marry through an app. Adonis was bored, but still glad that he was spending the night with her.

"She should not marry that guy! What's wrong with her? He's the one who stalked his ex and got arrested!" Chanel protested.

"You do know it's scripted, right?" Adonis asked.

"Yeah, but my human reactions aren't. Or do I exhaust you?" she asked.

He knew a trick question when he heard one.

"It was a factual though lazy comment," he replied.

"Thank you. Context matters," she said.

It was at that point that the show cut to a news story.

We are cutting our regular programming to bring you breaking news. The authorities have just confirmed that eight employees of Key-Tech Entertainment were found dead in a fire that engulfed their offices earlier tonight. Eyewitness reports state that there were explosions coming from the building before the fire ensued. Firefighters were able to put out the fire after two hours and no adjacent buildings were damaged. Although investigations are ongoing, it is suspected that it might have been caused by a gas leak. Unfortunately, several lives were lost in the tragedy. It is believed that the founder, Arnold Key, was among the dead. As police continue their investigations, we will bring....

Adonis listened to the news report with a funny sense of dread. He didn't know why, but he felt that a gas leak was a strange way for eight adults to go out.

"This story is wild," Chanel said.

"You can say that again," he replied.

"What were they doing in the office that late?"

"You have worked that late before, you know."

"What are the odds of a gas leak happening at Sephtis?" she posed.

"Hush! Don't say that," he ordered her.

"Oh? You believe in that speak it into existence nonsense?" she posed.

"It's not nonsense if it actually comes true," he said.

"It's never gonna happen, so relax," she said.

He frowned. She had no idea how gas leaks can happen when someone wants them to happen.

When he got back to the office the next morning, he was glad he had carried a change of clothes. It might have raised eyebrows if he hadn't managed to change, or if they arrived together. That's why he had left Chanel in bed. He was surprised to find Leroy seated at his desk.

"You're back! How are you feeling?" Adonis asked.

"I'm good. On medication, but I'll be fine," Leroy replied.

"Look, I'm really sorry about the cookies. I didn't know," Adonis said.

"It's fine. I should have warned you," Leroy said, then coughed slightly.

"Are you sure you're okay?"

"Yeah. I can't stay home even though the doctor wants me to. Not working makes me sick so I would rather be here," Leroy replied, "I can see everything is running fine."

"Yeah, everything's okay," Adonis said, inwardly praying that the code was masking itself as he had been told. Dmitri had managed to attach it to Chanel's records and manipulate the algorithm to plateau her sales. But he wasn't sure if the rest of the program would be affected. Adonis would keep checking on Leroy just to be sure.

"Whose album launch is tomorrow?" Leroy asked.

"Chanel's," Adonis replied.

"Oh great! She should hit the charts with a bang," Leroy said.

"I sure hope she does," Adonis said, knowing he was hoping for another outcome. But it was inevitable. Chanel was going to kill it.

He was right. The album launch the following night was one to behold. It was marketed well for a week, and because of Sephtis's reputation for great gigs and the popularity of Chanel's single, tickets sold out two days before the launch. Gunner had gone out of his way to set it up at the Atlantis

Resort, one the few five-star hotels in the Tropicon Islands. The tickets catered to the VVIP, VIP and the regular fans. Industry names were there, as well as eager fans. The resort put up a huge tent where the launch was happening. A red carpet led to it from the car park where the guests would arrive. There were special cushioned seats for all the guests, with ushers passing around complimentary drinks. The stage was set up well with glitzy props, lights, and a huge screen backdrop that relayed images during the performance. Banners with the company branding were at every strategic corner.

When all the seats were near full, the event started. Randy Rah, Bruce the Bermuda Triangle and Francine Mirrors all curtain-raised for her. Adonis saw the fruits of the choreography sessions, because they all put on great performances full of energy. They performed singles from their forthcoming albums, setting the tone for Chanel's arrival. She hit the stage in a captivating luminous blue outfit that reminded him of an old film, *Avatar*. It had large feathers trailing behind her that gave her the illusion of a majestic peacock. Carrying a customized guitar bought for her by Gunner, she strummed her way into people's hearts with the live band backing her up. It got so lively that the whole crowd was standing towards the end, waving their arms in the air and forcing her to repeat two of her songs. Those close to the stage threw cash notes at her. By the time she hit her last note on the guitar, the atmosphere was electrified. A standing ovation lasting several minutes followed. As Adonis watched, he had to say she was not the next Oceania; she was going to be bigger than Oceania.

After the event, the other artists in the Sephtis roster were backstage to pay their respects to Chanel. She was tired but still buzzing from the crowd's reception. Adonis could tell the other artists felt challenged. They were eager to have their album launches go as well or even better than hers. Their congratulations were also a way for them to get a bit of her magic, he mused. He hoped they would also be strong enough to accept when their shows didn't hit her high levels.

An hour later, Adonis and Chanel were standing outside Chanel's tour van. She was about to leave, and he was saying his goodbyes. Gunner walked up to them.

"Congratulations, superstar!" he said, hugging her. He had already done this immediately after the show. Seeing him do it again confirmed to Adonis that Gunner was very pleased.

"Thank you, Gunner!" Chanel replied.

"That strong start is good for the tour dates that are coming up," he said.

"You already locked them?" Chanel asked.

"It happened before you hit the stage. I just needed to see what kind of splash you made. I know you will light up that tour. Just keep the same energy," Gunner replied, "Check your email when you get to your room."

"All right. I will do that after I get some rest."

Gunner looked at Adonis.

"A.D., makes sure she gets to her hotel room. I don't want to find stories in the papers tomorrow that she hit the clubs," Gunner ordered.

"No worries, boss," Adonis replied.

"That's not even my scene!" Chanel protested.

"In my experience, it's never too late to start. I'm not taking chances. Travel safe!" Gunner said, as he turned and headed back into the auditorium.

"Well, I guess you will be my entertainment tonight. Once again," Chanel whispered with a cheeky wink.

↑

As Gunner walked through the empty tent, he smiled. It had been worth the investment. He had already struck four endorsement deals for Chanel before the show ended, and he knew a few more would be coming. The reporters he invited were swayed by her performance, although they still enjoyed the freebies he kept sending to their section to ensure they delivered glowing reviews. His tour locations already heard about how well it went and were eager to get her on the road. He knew he had to ride the wave, although it was her first tour. She was still young, she can handle it, he thought.

He dialed a number.

"He didn't come back tonight," Reggie said.

"He won't. He's spending another night at the hotel. You can wait for them there," Gunner replied.

"Okay, boss."

Gunner was hoping that Adonis's trip to see Oceania's family was out of grief. He needed to be sure. Human beings can be unpredictable.

↑

When they got to her hotel room, Adonis and Chanel took a shower then ate the takeaway dinner they'd bought on the way there. Thereafter they took some red wine, which Chanel loved. She was soon tipsy and convinced him to dance with her. She surprised him with her energy even after the launch performance. They then made out for some time but didn't go all the way. Finally, exhausted, they cuddled on her bed and passed out until the early hours of the morning.

When he woke up just as the sun peeked over the horizon, Adonis watched her sleep. She was the most beautiful woman he had seen, and the fact that he had spent the night in the same bed without taking her clothes off appealed to him even more. There was something special happening here, and he wanted to see how far it would go. First, he needed to get home and change.

As he left in a cab, he called Dmitri, who was still in bed.

"Why are you calling me now?" Dmitri asked.

"Rise and shine. It's time to get on the grind."

"Shut up, Addie. What do you want?"

"Listen. The launch last night was epic, man. Her numbers should be skyrocketing in the next few days. How are the numbers?"

"Addie, it's quarter to seven. I haven't woken up yet to check," Dmitri mumbled sleepily.

"Great. Okay, let me know as soon as you do. Also, this is the test for the program. I hope it doesn't act up and gets traced back to us."

"You need to chill. The rootkit is solid and masks itself well. So, you can breathe easy," Dmitri reassured him.

"I think she's going to pop. I'll get a better idea of the numbers when I reach the office."

"The program will work. Trust me," Dmitri said.

"Thanks. Let's talk soon."

Adonis hung up, more relaxed. If the code worked, it would buy him some time to figure out what to do. He had spotted the shark fins in the water. Now that her album was out, it was time to swim with the sharks.

CHAPTER THIRTEEN

"**S**HE'S GONE STRAIGHT to number one in the charts in the first week!" Leroy exclaimed.

"Oceania did that too," Vernon said, "The question is for how long she can stay there."

The two were standing in front of Leroy's computer, watching the numbers of Chanel's debut album sales rising in real time. Adonis, who was at his station, listened in.

"That's true, sir. I think she can stay there for a good while, if we use the music video you released as a marker. It hit one hundred million views in one week," Leroy replied.

Vernon grunted, unconvinced.

"Her sales numbers are still hovering over two million," he said.

"It's been growing at a steady ten percent per day," Leroy replied.

"It should be hitting thirty percent now. Especially after the launch," Vernon pointed out.

The eavesdropping Adonis was pleased. The rootkit was electronically limiting the growth trend, meaning the two men were looking at lower figures than the reality. It was working.

"I anticipate a snowball effect in the next three days. The initial burst was as high as forty percent, but it evens out sometimes to a lower percentage. Maybe we need to bump up the targeted marketing," Leroy said.

"Is he handling that?" Vernon asked, pointing at Adonis.

"Yes, he is handling some of it. Alongside Oceania's tribute album," Leroy replied.

"All right. Adonis, I want you to focus on the targeted marketing campaign for Chanel's album only for the next two days. Come up with something that will run on its own algorithm to roll out more sales volume for us. Spam them if you have to," Vernon instructed.

"Yes, sir. Although Leroy and I were going for a more organic approach with this, just to test the system," Adonis replied.

"The artists are on the other side of the door. In here, we are capitalists. We create the market we want by any means necessary. Organic is not our thing. Engineered is what makes this place tick. The sooner the two of you can understand that the faster you will grow our business. Understood?" Vernon said sternly.

"Understood," Leroy replied, casting a frown at Adonis.

"I'll get to it right away, sir," Adonis replied meekly.

When Gunner walked into Vernon's office, he found him

examining a miniature motorcycle. It was one of several dotting the office, which Vernon collected on his travels.

"Hello, boss," Gunner said.

"I watched the news. You created quite a spectacle. I was hoping that it would be just a page five article, not a headline. I'm not complaining though," Vernon remarked.

Gunner shrugged. "I figured destroying the place would be better than leaving the infrastructure for them to rebuild. They made the silly mistake of having their main server at the office."

"Now you understand why I wanted our main server away from here. Spread out the risk," Vernon said. "What are the streets saying?"

"They know it was a hit. I'm sure the police have done the autopsies and found the gunshot wounds on the bodies. But the clean-up crew did their job," Gunner said.

"I am counting on that, because I pay them that retainer for a reason," Vernon said.

"You saw the dossier I sent you? About the governor's deal?" Gunner asked.

"I saw it," Vernon replied.

"Key-Tech was giving him more than what we had offered. What do you think of it?"

"I can understand why he tried to go with Key-Tech. It's not really about the money," Vernon replied. He took the miniature motorcycle and pushed it slowly atop the desk.

"You should do a motocross event sometime. It would be good for the brand," Gunner said.

Vernon looked up and smiled. "You're right. I know a spot that can handle that. First, I want us to organize a meeting with the governor. It's time to get him to see the benefits of working with us."

"Wouldn't it be better to wait for the heat to cool off a bit?"

"There is no heat without us, Gunner. We are the heat," Vernon said.

Two days later, Gunner paid a visit to the FFX AI office for an update on Vernon's directive. Leroy had been pushing Adonis to rework the marketing approach. He knew when Gunner came to follow up things were serious.

"How are the numbers looking?" Gunner asked.

"Erm, yeah we have grown. Adonis has spammed more than twenty million possible clients within the target demographic, which was larger than the average. We are heading towards the three and a half million sales mark," Leroy replied.

"What's the percentage there?"

"That's gone up over twenty percent in the past two days," Leroy said.

Gunner nodded quietly.

"Are there any issues with the system that you have noticed?" Gunner asked.

"None. Works fine as always," Leroy said.

Gunner looked over at Adonis.

"A.D., did you notice any funny stuff with the system when Leroy was sick?"

"Nope. It was working fine," Adonis replied. He spoke as calmly as he could, because he noticed Gunner seemed restless.

"The boss told me you ramped up the marketing," Gunner said.

"Yes, sent out a higher volume than we usually do," Adonis replied.

"Okay. So why have we not hit thirty percent?"

"It's only been two days of work. Usually a week is a good time to see such growth," Leroy said.

"It was supposed to be thirty percent. Not twenty," Gunner insisted.

Adonis fidgeted, wondering where this was going. Was he going to be fired?

"We just need time. The market is unpredictable," Leroy said calmly.

"Well, the reason we have the AI system is to avoid unpredictability. We know what our clients want. We target those with disposable income, and we nail them fast. So, either you are not working or there's something wrong with the system," Gunner said.

Leroy and Adonis looked at each other.

"Well, which is it?" Gunner posed.

"We have stepped up our efforts. So, all we need is time," Leroy replied.

"All right. The system it is. I'm calling Nat," Gunner said, turning to leave.

"Gunner, we don't need Nat. Really," Leroy said.

"Don't worry. It's a quick checkup. Nothing big. Is checking our systems going to be a problem for you, Leroy?" Gunner asked as if daring him to challenge his decision.

Leroy gulped. "No, it will not be a problem."

"Good," Gunner said and left.

"Damn!" Leroy muttered. He ran his hands through his hair as he leaned back in his seat.

"Who is Nat?" Adonis asked.

"You don't want to know," Leroy replied.

"I actually do," Adonis said.

"Natasha Harper is the incognito version of FXX AI," Leroy said. "She runs the main server at a secret location away from here. She was also the lead architect of the whole system we are using right now."

"Sounds like someone inspiring," Adonis said.

"On paper. She's a bit of an asshole. It's not going to be pretty."

"What is she going to do?"

"She's going to check the whole system. I don't think she'll rip it apart. They want to keep the system running twenty-four seven. I think it's a waste of time and money. She doesn't come cheap. And I hate it when these guys' paranoia makes things expensive!"

Adonis's sense of dread was growing. "So, she's a computer genius, right?" he asked.

Leroy laughed sarcastically. "You could say that. If there were mercenaries in the tech world, she would be the mascot. She does things in the tech world that you could only dream of," Leroy replied.

Adonis felt his chest tighten. He needed to get out of there.

"Do you need water or something?" he asked Leroy.

"No, I'm fine," Leroy replied.

"Let me get something to drink. I'll be back in a few," Adonis said as he left.

Adonis headed straight for the balcony, his phone itching in his hand. He needed to call Dmitri.

"Hey, what's up?" a cheery Dmitri asked.

"What are you up to?"

"I'm checking out your album numbers. This girl is going to be a millionaire at this rate!"

"Listen. Something has come up. They are bringing someone in to check the system," Adonis said.

"Who's this someone?"

"Leroy says its someone who helped build the system. Although Gunner said it's going to be just a quick checkup, I don't know how good they are. They might find this thing," Adonis replied.

"Aah. I wouldn't sweat it. I told you that thing is invisible. Chill," Dmitri tried to reassure him.

"Don't play with me, this is serious," Adonis warned.

"I'm serious too. I know what I'm talking about. My brother Kai vouched for it so relax," Dmitri replied.

Adonis took a deep sigh then hung up. He took a few minutes in the sun before going back in.

When Natasha arrived, everyone knew about it, although not everyone knew who she was. Adonis, who was coming from the studio at the time, listened as people gossiped. Some people whispered that she was a rock music artist there to visit Vernon. Others assumed she was a visual artist commissioned to redesign the FFX office. The only people who knew her real mission were Vernon, Gunner, Leroy, and Adonis. The bosses were okay with that because it was a way for them to protect her. She was an asset.

She arrived by helicopter, which landed on the large lawn adjacent to the Sephtis office. Adonis understood two things from this: the company spent big on her to come through for them on short notice, and Natasha didn't live on the Tropicon Islands.

Reminiscent of the classic *Matrix* movies, Natasha was dressed in an all-black coat, shirt, trousers, and boots. The only thing that was different from the look in the movies was she didn't wear any sunglasses. Instead, she had green contact lenses and multi-colored braids, which she tied up in a bun atop her scalp.

Adonis could understand why people likened her to rock music or visual art. She probably liked both anyway, but it wasn't a conversation he would have with her. She marched through the office lobby headed to the FFX office, flanked by Gunner and one of his henchmen. She meant business, and as Adonis watched her disappear into the FFX office, he had a feeling of dread.

⚑

Gail and Marissa sat on Marissa's bed, hanging out. It was mid-morning and they were both still in their pajamas. Only a year and some months apart in age, they had developed the habit when they were younger on the weekends or public holidays. They would sleep in or wake up early and talk about anything under the sun. They became the best of friends and knew everything about each other. However, this practice had become less frequent as they got older and became more aware of themselves and their bodies.

The gap that had developed between them became glaring after Gail's overdose. Marissa had no idea her sister was taking drugs, nor understood why. She was understandably shocked that the sister she considered her best friend had kept this secret from her. In an effort to make up for lost ground, Marissa had become intentional. Initially, she would spend time with her sister when she got back from school. But as her recovery got harder, Marissa took a few days off school to help her mother and Dmitri get Gail back on her feet. Her mother had argued against it, but it was still early in the school term, so she wasn't going to fall too far behind.

She would often get to Gail's room during the withdrawal days when it was hardest. She would watch her scream, rant, itch, and break down until eventually the symptoms started subsiding. By that time, their bond had grown stronger as Gail realized that her sister would always be there for her. One thing that was still plaguing Gail was insomnia, and today she had sought her sister out after a restless night.

"I just kept waking up in a cold sweat. Over and over and over again," Gail said, her right arm circling in the air to describe her emotion.

"But why were you dreaming about the black dog? It's a scoundrel," Marissa said. The black dog they were talking about was a well-known stray dog in the neighborhood.

"It's a scoundrel yes, but have you never wondered who owns it? Why it's always around the corner store? Why it always stares at you as if it knows you?"

Marissa laughed.

"It's not funny sis!" Gail exclaimed, taking the pillow, and hitting her with it. They were soon engaged in a pillow fight, with loud screams and laughs.

"Are we going to need another set of pillows for both of you?" Terek's loud voice boomed at the two girls and they stopped their play abruptly, still giggling. He was standing at the door, which he held ajar.

"No, Dad! This is just good old fun!" Gail said.

"Can I come in?" he asked.

"Sure!" Gail said, as the two girls settled back down on the bed.

Terek stepped into the room and went to lean on one bedroom wall.

"It's good to see the both of you so happy," he said.

"It's good to have you home too. That pillow fight got me going. Who wants a banana or something? I'm headed to the kitchen," Gail said, standing up.

"Get me three cookies," Marissa said.

"And you, Dad?" Gail asked.

"Get me the same," he replied.

"Cool! I'll be back in a minute," Gail said, as she bounded off.

Terek looked at Marissa, who was working her laptop. He moved to the bed and sat down.

"Everything okay, Marissa?" he asked.

"Yeah! Sure," she replied with a smile, "just looking for a series to watch now."

"It's one of those mornings, eh?" he said.

"Yeah, life is meant to be lived," Marissa said.

"Gotcha," he replied.

He knew it would take him a while to get into a good rhythm of conversation around the house, but at least he was trying, and they were open to connect. Terek felt a gentle gust blow in from the window. He looked up and saw it was open and remembered the night he arrived.

"Does the streetlight outside the house always flicker?" he asked.

"Yeah it does that every so often when it feels like it. Don't know why. Mom asked the property management guys to come fix it and they've taken forever," Marissa replied, her eyes fixed on her computer screen.

"They're like that everywhere in the country, not just here," he said.

"I bet you've got stories," she replied.

"Yeah I do. I just found it odd that it was doing that the night I arrived. It hasn't misbehaved since," he said.

"Might be a good sign or a bad one? Who knows," Marissa replied with a laugh.

"I also saw someone else that night. Jumping out of this beautiful window you got here," Terek said. Marissa's head froze, and she slowly looked up at him.

"You saw that?"

"Yeah. It was a little late for her to be leaving your room, right?"

"I guess," Marissa replied, caution in her voice.

"Who was she, Marissa?"

Marissa fidgeted a little.

"A good friend of mine," she replied.

Terek was even more curious now. He wanted to know more without pushing her away.

"You know if it's a drugs thing—" he started.

"It's got nothing to do with drugs!" Marissa interrupted.

"Sorry, I take that back," he said. After a pause, he continued. "So, she's a friend. Or more than a friend?"

Marissa sighed as she figured out her answer. He waited patiently.

"She's more than a friend," Marissa whispered. Terek nodded knowingly.

"How long has this been going on?" he asked.

"About six months. Look, I don't need Mom knowing about this."

"When would you like to tell her?"

"When I'm ready. Please, don't tell her. If you do…"

He put an arm on her shoulder.

"Hey, it's me, your dad. I'm here to support you, okay? We'll tell her when you're ready," he said.

Just then, Gail came back with the goodies on a large plate.

"Sweet tooth coming through!" she exclaimed.

As she placed the plate on the bed, she noticed their serious expressions.

"Who died?" Gail asked.

"No one! Pass me them cookies!" Marissa said, holding out her hand.

"I have a story about the time I ate some cookies before a show and regretted it," Terek said with a smile.

"Let's hear it!" Gail said.

They were soon laughing about Terek's escapades.

🌴

Adonis wasn't looking forward to getting home. He was tired but wished he could spend the evening with Chanel. The nights were relatively peaceful when he stayed in her hotel room. Dmitri had called it the honeymoon phase before the storm, but Adonis didn't see it that way. With the energy they created whenever they were together, Adonis could see himself making babies with this girl. Although he meant that as a phrase because he wasn't keen on having kids now.

He walked in and found Terek alone in the living room,

watching television. Adonis walked past him, heading for his bedroom.

"How was your day?" Terek asked.

For some reason, Adonis stopped. "Now you care?" Adonis posed.

"I have always cared," Terek replied.

Adonis walked up to the couch where Terek sat. "I didn't hear you ask me that question in the last five years."

"Well I did try to talk to you on the phone but—"

"On the phone? You think video calls and text messages make you a father?" Adonis fumed.

"Don't raise your tone when talking to me, boy!" Terek snapped, getting on his feet so that they were now looking at each other. Adonis could look him in the eye, because their height difference was marginal.

"Or what? Huh? What are you going to do about it?" Adonis asked.

He didn't have to wait to find out. Terek's fist was already flying to meet Adonis's head as soon as he finished his sentence. Adonis ducked, but he wasn't fast enough. Terek connected with his cheek, leaving a stinging bruise. As he ducked, Adonis already knew his counter, aiming his punch towards Terek's mid-section. He connected well enough to make the older man lean forward in pain, leaving his face exposed. Adonis went to work, landing a right and left hook. Terek reeled into the couch, collapsing onto it.

Before Adonis could close in for the kill, his mother and sisters were on him, pulling him back from his stricken father.

"Stop it, Addie! Will you stop it?" Bernice shouted at him.

"He came at me! A grown man attacking his son! That's pathetic!" Adonis shouted.

"Stop it, Addie! Why did you have to hit him back?" Bernice asked. Adonis turned to look at his mother in genuine bewilderment.

"So, you're taking his side now?" he asked.

"I'm taking no one's side. Get a grip on yourself!"

"Nah, I'm out of here," Adonis said, and stormed out into the night.

CHAPTER FOURTEEN

WHEN HE STORMED out, Adonis didn't know where to go. He just needed to get away. He wasn't going to spend the night at Chanel's room. He wouldn't have minded it, but he also was not in the right headspace at that time, nor was he willing to tell her about life at home. For some reason, he hadn't gotten comfortable enough to tell her more about his family. He also didn't want to head to Dmitri's for similar reasons. Although Dmitri knew his father was back, he didn't know about the tensions between the two of them. Crashing at his place was out of the question. Adonis resolved to walk around the block a few times until he calmed down.

Two hours later, he went back home and slept away. When he woke up the next morning, he didn't have the usual anger knotting his insides. Beating up his father was a milestone he subconsciously wanted. He admitted to himself that the memory of the winded man lying on the couch had been satisfying.

At breakfast that morning they sat across each other and ate with everyone else, the first time that had happened without a showdown. They didn't address each other and no one at the table raised the fight that had happened the previous night. Strangely, Adonis didn't mind this new dynamic. He might just have room to start tolerating Terek's prolonged presence.

As Adonis left the house, his phone rang. It was Dmitri.

"Bro, are you at the office?" Dmitri asked.

"Not yet why?"

"Oh boy. I guess your system support person found us," Dmitri said.

"What? I thought you said they couldn't?" Adonis asked.

"Well, nothing is foolproof. She found the rootkit and disabled it. The numbers on my end are back to the real figures."

"You mean you can still see the system interface?"

"Yeah, but I can't do anything about it anymore. At least for the time being. There's a window to try and reactivate it in seventy-two hours but it depends with how long your guy will be up there," Dmitri replied.

"It's not a guy. It's a woman," Adonis clarified.

"It's a woman? She's ace! Who is this?"

"Natasha Harper."

"That name sounds familiar. Anyway, just wanted to give you a heads up."

"So, you're saying the safety is off?"

"Yeah. It is what it is," Dmitri said. "One more thing: Chanel's numbers were already past the nine million sales mark. Do with that information what you will."

As he increased his walking pace to work, Adonis knew they were going to activate Chanel's kill switch soon and he could do nothing to stop it. It felt hollow in the pit of his stomach.

↑

When Adonis arrived at the office, he found Natasha seated on Leroy's seat, working away. True to his earlier assumption, she was listening to rock music from a small portable speaker.

Leroy on the other hand had brought in a seat from the common rooms and was watching her, looking visibly bored.

"You're here early," Leroy said to Adonis.

"I could say the same," Adonis said with a smile, "How's it going with this?"

"Nat fixed it," Leroy replied.

"For real? You fixed it up?" Adonis asked her.

"Yeah! It wasn't easy. Seems there was a glitch with the back end of the system," Natasha replied, her voice husky and casual.

"A glitch?" Adonis asked.

"Yeah. Some small error with the code means that it wasn't generating the readings as accurately as the data coming in."

"Oh. So, it was it something that was there in the beginning?" Adonis asked.

"It actually wasn't," Vernon said. Adonis spun to see his boss standing behind him. Adonis was startled but quickly composed himself.

"It was apparently something that has happened on Leroy's watch," Vernon asserted.

Adonis was nervous now but tried to keep it as invisible as

possible. What did they know? Did they track it to him? How would he get out of there if things went downhill?

"I wouldn't have known," Leroy said defensively.

"Is that so? How about the two of you come with me. Let's have a little chat," Vernon said. Leroy and Adonis looked at each other briefly. They then got up and walked to the door.

Vernon grilled them separately in his office, starting with Leroy. He was keen to know if Leroy had noticed any patterns to indicate that the system was compromised. Leroy hadn't noticed anything, and he stuck to that story. Adonis gave that same response, although he got the impression that Vernon didn't believe either of them. This was more evident by the fact that when he left for home after an unusual workday, Natasha was still at Leroy's station. She was going nowhere.

When Adonis got home later that day, his mother had a surprising story for him.

"You know, I was at the shopping center today, and I felt like I was being followed," Bernice his mother said.

"What made you think that?" Adonis asked.

"There was a black car that kept showing up in our rear-view mirror. I didn't notice it, but Terek did since he was driving me around. We thought it might be the cops or something," she said.

Adonis turned to his father: "Is there something you did out there that we need to know about?"

"Come on, I'm not like that anymore," Terek said.

"If you're here to lay low then I think you need to think of leaving soon," Adonis muttered.

"I told you, It's not me! Drinking, gambling, and dealing are all behind me! I'm here, just as I am. Why don't you wanna listen? Don't my actions say something to you?" Terek protested.

Adonis paused for thought. Terek did have a point. Adonis had a heightened suspicion of him, and maybe this was blinding him. Other than the bust-up they'd had and his lazing around, he hadn't seen anything of concern from Terek. He was also offering the benefit of doubt because he had his own secrets now.

"So, you thought it's the cops? Did they follow you home?" Adonis asked Terek.

"They basically did. But they didn't stake out, they just drove on once we got here. It was weird," Terek said.

Adonis rubbed his chin. It was concerning. Something was afoot, and it was probably Gunner behind it. He didn't like the feeling of walls closing in, but the signs were there.

"If we notice something tonight, we have to call the cops," Adonis said. He then went to sit on the front porch, watching the street. Should he tell them what's going on at the office? He felt it was too early to tell. But when would be the right time though?

There was nothing unusual on the street – just two young men walking a dog, a couple in their fifties taking a walk and a young couple lazily strolling. The street had a few cars, but they were all familiar. Everything looked normal, except the blinking streetlight. It oddly reminded him of a siren. Like a warning light.

↑

Natasha Harper was buzzing on coffee and energy drink.

The doctor had told her that this combo was responsible

for her irregular heart rhythms. Her defiant solution was cutting the frequency from daily use to when firefighting client emergencies. She had also lowered the dosage of energy drink in the mix, because that was the chemical-laden bit that caused complications, she rationalized.

It still gave her heart a good pump, and she walked around more soon after taking the concoction. But she needed it these days. When she was younger, she could go for days without sleep. These days, in her forties, she had to pace herself more or get a boost drink like this one.

She liked the big money clients like Sephtis because they knew her worth. Back when she had to be an anonymous hacker, she made money but not as much. Her worth was not known, so she had to haggle often to get the rate that came close to being decent, but even then, it didn't match her skills. She was a one of a kind woman, her fellow hackers would say. She went by the name Pandora, after the first woman in Greek mythology.

She had quit criminal hacking two decades ago in 2008, after the banking fraud scandal. The authorities of several countries almost tracked her down and that was too close for comfort. She decided to reinvent herself. She changed her name from Sarah Jones to Natasha Harper and went public. She started building artificial intelligence systems that no one else was doing. She saw the future, and by the time everyone had caught on, she was one of the leading names in the business. But she didn't run a multi-million-dollar company. She didn't care for large staffing and tall skyscrapers. She was the business, and if you wanted her, you had better match her worth.

When she found the rootkit in the FXX AI system, she

knew it was not an outside hack. Someone had put it in there, which narrowed the options to either Leroy or Adonis. This is what she had told Vernon.

She also renegotiated a higher fee when she was asked to track the external server that was running the rootkit. That's why she was spending the night working, because she loved the hunt. It was like a Bengal tiger hiding in the trees. Your prey can't see or hear you coming, and that power of stealth made her feel like a rock star.

🌴

Gunner drove up to the second floor of the storied parking. There were very few cars, so it was easy to get a spot. Five minutes later, the white saloon car of his informant came into view in his rear-view mirror. The car parked on the opposite side of the parking garage.

Gunner got out of his car and walked across the distance to the white saloon. "You asked to see me," Gunner said to the driver, who had lowered his tinted window halfway.

"Yeah. How's it going with the deal?" the informant asked.

"It's going," Gunner replied.

"Good to hear," the informant replied.

"I thought I said you are not supposed to get in touch with me. Our business was concluded," Gunner said.

"Yeah. It's just that I'm a little low on cash, and I want to get off the island for a bit. You know, lay low," the man replied.

"Once you gave me the chip, our business ended. Or are you getting heat on your end?" Gunner asked.

"I haven't seen anything. But you never know. It would be

a shame if they caught me and my stomach is still rumbling," the man joked.

Gunner bit his lip and looked around the garage. Noting that the coast was clear, he reached into the car and grabbed the man's neck in a crushing chokehold. The man writhed in pain as he tried to punch away Gunner's right hand. But Gunner's thick arm was built for this, gifted with a vice-like grip. Three minutes later, the man was limp. Gunner kept the hold for a little while longer until he started feeling the body getting cold. He released his hold, and the man slumped on his steering wheel. Gunner took out a sanitary wipe and swabbed the man's neck several times.

He then walked over to his car and drove off.

🌴

Adonis was impatient. He kept looking through the living room window at the street outside, just in case there were strange cars or people moving about. His mother Bernice was knitting as Terek read a magazine.

"You need to settle down, Addie," Bernice said.

Adonis looked at her. She didn't get the weight of his worry. Maybe he needed to tell her. "Ma, there have been a few strange things going on at work and I don't know if this is connected."

"What strange things? And what do you have to do with it?" Bernice asked with concern.

"I started suspecting that they are harming their artists, so I started looking out for things," Adonis said.

"What do you mean harming their artists?" Terek asked, looking up from his reading.

"Killing them," Adonis said.

His mother gasped, and Terek lowered the magazine to his lap. "I've never heard of such a thing," Terek said.

"Are you trying to lose your job, son?" his mother asked.

"I'm just keeping an eye out, trying to prove the story. Maybe the people you saw were not looking for you," he replied.

"Then who were they looking for?" she asked.

"I don't know. But like I said, if my theory is true, that they are killing their artists, why would you not believe me?"

"Your father is in the music business and he's never heard of this kind of thing," she replied.

Adonis stared at Terek, who looked back at him.

"I may not have seen it, but it doesn't make it totally impossible. Adonis might be on to something. But I just don't see why they would come for us," he replied.

"Because it's possible they suspect me. That I know something," Adonis replied.

"I think you're overreacting, boy. You don't have evidence," Terek said.

Adonis's eyes turned black. "You're so consistent, aren't you?" Adonis asked him.

"Let's not start," Terek said.

"No, let's do it! You want to be 'Dad' so much but don't have any evidence backing that title. Yet you want me to provide evidence?"

"He's your father, Addie! You can't change that!" Bernice said.

Adonis laughed mockingly. "If he were my father, wouldn't he have wanted me to be a father as well? You remember taking away my kid, 'Dad'?" Adonis asked.

"You were sixteen for crying out loud!" Terek bellowed.

"You went behind my back, paid off Alesha's parents so that she could abort our baby! You had no right, you piece of shit!" Adonis exclaimed.

"It's in the past Addie, forget about it," Bernice pleaded.

"It was my baby, Ma. Don't you see that?" an emotional Adonis asked.

"I see it, Addie. I see it. I'm sorry," she said.

Bernice looked at Terek, who sat there defiantly.

"I did what I had to do to protect you! Look at you now, going onwards to making your name in the industry. You think that would have been possible if you were saddled with a baby? No! I saved your ass from destruction!" Terek shouted back.

"I didn't need saving! Ma needed saving! My sisters needed saving! We all needed a father and not a hobo pretending to be a creative genius!" Adonis retorted.

They both went silent, heaving with emotion.

"You both need to stop this. It's tearing me apart," a tearful Bernice said.

Adonis shook his head. He never wanted to see his mother in pain. But he didn't know how to reconcile his emotions for the man that had ruined their lives. He also realized at that moment; how helpless he was. He didn't really know how to save Chanel, nor how to make his family believe him. He was at a loss.

He slowly walked out of the living room towards his room. He needed to sleep on it. Maybe tomorrow, if they were still alive, he would have an answer for everything, including what it means to forgive. Because, at that very moment, he didn't know what forgiveness meant.

He also dreaded waking up the next day. It would be the

first day of Chanel's tour, and he didn't feel like he was ready for the rollercoaster ride that was to come.

↑

Dancing as if he was still in his clubbing days, Dmitri was in the zone. The Caribbean music pumped through the house as he danced to the beat while biting into a weed cookie. It was helping him forget the failure of the rootkit.

He sat down to check the numbers on the FFX AI interface. He was surprised that they hadn't cut him off yet, which was why he held on to the hope he could reactivate it to limit the album sales. True to Adonis's words, Chanel's debut album was raking in the numbers.

It was as he was sipping on his soda that a dark chat window popped up in front of him. He stared at it in surprise. It was a simple blank screen, with a white blinking cursor. He carefully placed the soda down. He had only seen it being used by Kai when chatting with other hackers, but he had never used it himself.

He was about to close the window when a text appeared.

Hello. Are you there?

Dmitri hesitated, unsure if he should respond. Who was this?

Yes, I am. Who is this? Dmitri typed.

A friend. How are the numbers looking?

Dmitri paused. He was racking his brain. It wasn't Adonis, he was sure.

They're looking good. Why?

The cursor blinked for a few seconds before the reply came.

I think they are better than what you were showing us.

Dmitri was catching on. It was Natasha Harper. His heart rate increased. Before he could type back, another text came in:

You think I wouldn't notice? Pretty good work.

Dmitri didn't know what to do. He tried to close the pop-up window, but it wouldn't respond to his mouse prompts.

You must be trying to shut this window. The fact that you can't means one thing:

Dmitri paused as he waited for the blinking cursor to add new text.

I am in control now. I know who you are. Stay safe, Dmitri.

The chat window disappeared, just as abruptly as it had come.

He realized the numbers he was seeing were no longer moving. When he tried to navigate the system, he was denied access at every turn. He was shut out. The operation was over.

"Shit!" Dmitri cursed, banging the table in front of him. The impact sent the glass of soda toppling to the floor and onto the carpet. The stain started spreading. Dmitri watched it, and for some reason it looked to him like blood.

"Shit!"

He quickly shut down the computer and started unplugging it from the wall. In fifteen minutes, he had packed his server into a box, alongside every hard drive and important material he could find. He added to that some t-shirts, jeans and jackets into a bag. Before he left the house, he set his nanny cams on. He then locked up and left.

As he drove his Oldsmobile down the road, he had no idea when he would come back. But he knew he had to lay low for as long as possible, because he definitely had a target on his back.

CHAPTER FIFTEEN

THE TOUR BUS sped down the highway. It was blue in color with gold and yellow highlights and bore large chrome-plated wheels. On each side was Chanel's image and the graphic text 'Chanel – the Dream Tour', and it created buzz wherever it went. It rode in a convoy of five cars: the first car was of the logistics and security team while the second was Gunner's SUV. The tour bus was third in line, followed by the makeup and wardrobe van and lastly another security team vehicle. They were pre-booked in the best hotels in each location they visited, although occasionally Chanel wanted to sleep in the tour bus. She loved the thing because it was cozy and very comfortable. It was designed for that, a luxury bus with everything you needed: it had a kitchen with necessary appliances and foodstuffs, a toilet and hot shower, a TV lounge and a chilling lounge where Chanel liked to spend most of her time. The lounge was decked out with padded leather seats, warm rugs and great interior touches to make it feel like home. Finally, the chilling lounge converted into a double bunk bedroom when night fell, with no problem with heating because it had its own battery supply for those chilly nights. Sephtis was serious about this aspect of things, unlike other companies in the area who were now playing catch-up.

They were headed to their third show at the Gum Tree Arena, a five-hour ride away. The first two shows had gone very well. The first one had a few empty seats but a great responsive crowd. The second venue was sold out, and they expected that trend to continue right up to their eighth and final show. Chanel was the natural performer Adonis had imagined. She had stage presence, could dance, play with a band, play three instruments and above all, sing. Fans were very keen on that; can you sing as well live as you do on the record? Each time, she got resounding ovations. She was quite excited heading to the next show.

"I'm not sure what this fame thing is, but I think I'm beginning to see it," she said to him.

"You haven't encountered fame yet. But this is how it feels on your way there," he replied.

"I don't think I want to get there. This is a better place to be," Chanel said.

"You're no longer in control of that. The fans are," Adonis remarked.

Adonis kept checking on his family often. So far, nothing unusual had happened. He had tried reaching Dmitri, but his phone was not going through for some reason. Adonis hoped it was just another of his disappearances into the coding world. He would resurface soon. But the thought kept nagging at him.

🌴

The fan that was spinning in the governor's office made a slight creaking sound with each revolution. It was on slow speed mode, Vernon figured, so the frequency of the creak was not high enough to make him want to rip it out of the ceiling. It did irritate him all the same.

He was seated across from the governor, who was twiddling his thumbs as he read a document on Vernon's tablet. Save for the shaggy gray hair on his head, Governor Harris looked sharp dressed in a trim pinstripe suit and tie, which Vernon felt was quite a good thing for a corrupt man. At least he had good taste to show for the millions he stole.

"You're asking for a lot more than our last conversation and offering me less. Am I reading the right document?" asked Governor Harris.

"Yes, you are. To the last detail," Vernon replied.

"I think you already know I'm going to turn down this proposal. Not just because it is offensive, but I am still reviewing the tender applications for the monopoly license."

"Well, we both know the review ended weeks ago. Too bad the winners of that race encountered an unfortunate accident," Vernon said casually.

The Governor pursed his lips. "We do have other names short listed to take their place."

"I think it would be wise for you to put our name at the top of that list. The offer aside, we have more tech and infrastructure than all our competitors combined," Vernon stated.

"This was never about the size of the bidding companies but about the welfare of the artists and communities they live in," Harris replied.

Vernon laughed. "Cut the bullshit, old man. The deal in front of you is what you need to focus on. The politics will take care of itself."

"And if I don't?"

"I admire your career. You have been here for ten years. If I remember correctly in the last election, you ran on the ticket of family values and restoring national dignity. I can relate to that. My father taught the same thing. Do you know I voted for you?" Vernon asked.

"I know that Vernon, and appreciate your support, but—"

"Sorry, I wasn't finished yet," Vernon interrupted, "So it will be interesting to see your voters' reaction to things their governor has been up to down at the Strip Resorts. Especially the presidential suite. I'm sure a lot of parents in the community will be concerned to know their teenage daughters have been your guests there several times. Just swipe left on the tablet."

He watched the old man swiping left. Several images appeared to him, each one more graphic than the former. The old man started sweating as he struggled to find a response.

"Would you like some water, sir? Should I turn up the fan?" Vernon offered in mild amusement.

Ten minutes later, he left with the monopoly license that would take Sephtis into the next stratosphere of business and data mining. Every entertainment company in the Tropicon Islands territory was now under his thumb. His father would have been impressed.

🌴

Chanel's third show at the Gum Tree Arena was a full house

and one of her best performances. She was even forced to go past her one-hour live set when fans asked for encores, which she obliged. She was building a great following as one of the best live acts to break into the scene and it was refreshing, Adonis observed.

As she cooled off in the changing room, Adonis went outside to where they had parked the tour bus. He always scanned the area to make sure there were no groupies hanging around the place. Chanel hadn't hit that level of fame yet, but he expected it. He had fended off a lot of groupies around Oceania's shows. It was a safety issue; no one wanted to see a stranger with other motives close to your talented artist while on tour.

After confirming that the coast was clear, he texted Chanel that she could come out when ready. As he waited, he called back home.

His mother's phone rang for longer that it usually did.

"Hello, Bernice's phone," Terek's voice came through the earpiece.

Adonis sighed. He was not keen on talking to Terek, but he had to see if they were okay.

"Hello, Terek. Is Mom there?"

"She's in the shower. You want to leave a message?"

"Yeah. You can tell her to call me back when she can."

"All right. Is everything okay?"

"Yeah. Anything strange happening there?" Adonis asked.

"Nothing so far," Terek replied.

"If something happens you should think of going somewhere. My Aunt Grace lives near the research base. You can crash there for a few days," Adonis suggested.

"I don't think that will be necessary. I'll look out for her," Terek said.

"Look Terek, this is not the time to be naïve."

"Why are we moving? We have done nothing wrong," Terek asserted.

Adonis had heard enough. "Just tell Mom to call me," Adonis said, and hung up.

That had agitated him. After a long day, it's the last thing he needed. He wished he could be back home; he would have forced them into it somehow. The one person who could speak some sense to the family was Dmitri. He dialed him up. Again, the call wasn't going through. He hadn't responded to the text sent earlier. What was going on?

"Hello, stranger," a sultry voice came from the shadows.

He turned to see a freshened-up Chanel, free from the stage clothes, walk up to him. She was wearing her charmer's smile. He forced himself to warm up to it.

"Hey there," he said, as they exchanged short, passionate kisses. "How are you feeling?"

"Fantastic!" she replied. "I think live performances are becoming my drug. I thought they would drain me, but they fire me up a good one."

"Is that so?" he asked.

"Yeah it is... How about we do a quick one to celebrate before the driver comes to take us away?"

She drew closer to him and kissed him some more.

Moments later they were all over each other in the tour bus's cozy lounge seat. She was on top of him, her desire making her grope him as she showered kisses on his lips. She then traced his body with her lips, starting from his neck, heading towards his chest. She was just about to start unbuttoning his short when they both heard a knock on the bus's door.

"Chanel! Are you in there?" Gunner bellowed as the door came open at the same time.

With quick reflexes, Adonis lifted himself and Chanel up to a sitting position. He was busy straightening his shirt as Chanel grabbed one of the throw pillows. Gunner came in and paused, as if he had noticed something but he was not too sure what.

"Am I interrupting something?" Gunner asked.

"Nope, nothing. We were just vibing, that's all," Chanel quickly said.

"Vibing, huh?" Gunner asked.

"Anything to help me calm down after the show," Chanel said. Adonis was impressed by her improvisation.

Gunner shrugged. "Whatever rocks your boat. I forgot to tell you at the debrief I need you tomorrow morning at eleven. We have a live Q and A with some fans."

"For real? I can't sleep in?"

"If you stop the vibing, you might get close to eight hours of sleep in. Your choice. Don't be late," Gunner replied, eyeing both of them. "Goodnight, kids."

With that, he left.

The two lovebirds looked at each other, their longing still alive. They would have pursued it some more, but the tour bus driver came back.

"Let's ride people!" the driver shouted.

"Do you expect to keep wearing my clothes here or are you planning to go back for more? They won't fit you," Kai said.

A hulk of a man, Kai towered above Dmitri's average height as he sipped on his can of beer. Dmitri smiled, amused by the question.

"You know I don't have a thing for cut off t-shirts and leather pants, so you don't have to worry about that," Dmitri replied.

"There's always a first time," Kai replied.

"Nah. That will mean that I'm letting them win. Never happening," Dmitri said.

They both laughed.

"So, you think they know where you live," Kai asked.

"I know they do. That's what the text suggested anyway," Dmitri replied.

"They must be having a good hacker with them then," his brother said, "My boys rode past your place earlier today but didn't see anything."

"I haven't seen anything remotely either," Dmitri said, referring to the nanny cams, "But it doesn't mean they won't try something."

Kai nodded.

"Well if they do, then they better be ready for some heat," Kai said. He took his last sip of beer and crushed the can in his hand.

Dmitri hoped that would be the case because he had nowhere else to go.

↑

It was after the third show on their eight-concert tour that Adonis told her.

They were having dinner in Chanel's tour bus, eating

takeout from a restaurant they had discovered. It was just the two of them.

"You know, there are a couple of artists signed to the Sephtis roster who have died the last couple of years," he said.

"Oh? Other than Oceania?" Chanel asked.

"Yeah, other than Oceania. About three others have died while signed on the label," he replied.

"Damn! Is this an urban legend story you're try to create here? The Secret Curse of Sephtis?" she asked cheekily.

"No, it's not my kind of thing. I was just curious," he said. "But they all died soon after they blew up."

Chanel shrugged. "It happens a lot. Tupac, Biggie. Then the album sales go through the roof for years after," she said.

"Exactly," he replied. He went quiet, just to confirm that she had caught on.

"Oh, you think that will happen to me?" Chanel asked.

"Yeah."

Chanel laughed hard, so much that she started coughing as some food went the wrong way. He expected the reaction, but it still angered him.

"It's not a joke! Something odd about the whole thing is that once their album sales hit ten million, they soon died. Every single one. Don't you find that weird?" he posed.

She shrugged. "I don't know, man. Speaking of weird, it's interesting you haven't noticed that I have eaten three drumsticks back to back."

"I actually have. You have strong cravings sometimes."

"Not like this one. This is different. Wanna guess why?" she asked, giving a wink.

"I have no idea," he replied.

Chanel leaned forward.

"It's been seven days since my last period," she whispered.

"Wait, what?" Adonis asked. Chanel gave him a wry smile.

"What do you think?" she asked.

"You can't be... No way..."

"Are you disappointed?"

"No! Hell no! If you're not playing me, then wow. That's amazing!" he said, and hugged her tight. He was surprised by how happy he was by the news they might be having a baby.

They did two more shows, and Chanel aced them both. Adonis was more paranoid about her every move, checking in regularly. He took it further by watching for strangers around her and banning groupies from the backstage. It got so serious that Chanel had to talk to him.

"What's up with you A.D.?" she asked.

"What are you talking about?"

"Can you give me some breathing space? You're always up in my business!" Chanel lamented.

"I'm doing what I have to do," he replied.

"No, I don't think you have to."

He grabbed her shoulders and made sure she was facing him.

"Don't you see I'm trying to protect you?" he asked.

For the first time she could see genuine fear in his eyes. She couldn't ignore that.

"I've been thinking about what you said," Chanel mumbled. "I believe you."

Adonis looked into her eyes and felt relieved. "I could prank you, but that's not something I would joke about," he said.

"What do we do about it?"

"I have a plan I've been thinking about the last couple of days. But I'll need your help."

"I'm ready when you are," she replied.

↑

At the end of the sixth show, they put their plan to action.

Gunner, who always insisted on a debrief meeting after each show, called for one in the backstage changing room as usual.

"Gunner, why don't we do it in the tour bus this time?" Chanel suggested.

"Why there?" Gunner asked.

"Well, I got this really great bottle of vodka I wanted to bust open to celebrate how far we have come."

"The tour is not over," Gunner stated.

"What Chanel is trying to say is that we have so far had a good run. We performed in front of a total of fifty thousand fans!" Adonis said.

Chanel chimed in: "I have never done that. No one in Sephtis has ever done that. It calls for us to celebrate!"

Gunner came around to their thinking and agreed. At the tour bus, Adonis opened the bottle then proceeded to pour into the glasses away from Gunner's gaze. He served the drinks as they discussed what worked and didn't work in the show as usual. Ten minutes after he took his first sip, Gunner fell over from his seat and collapsed to the floor, unconscious. Adonis rushed to him and checked his pulse. His heart was beating. He estimated the crushed sleeping pill he had added to the drink would knock him out for about two hours, but he wasn't sure: the pill and alcohol were not a safe bet.

He and Chanel gathered what they could and took off into the night, hoping to get as far away as possible before Vernon and his men started hunting for them.

CHAPTER SIXTEEN

ADONIS AND CHANEL hitchhiked a ride from a friendly truck driver all the way back to the city, which was a lengthy ride but worth it. They had switched off their phones as soon as they had escaped. They didn't know how long Gunner would be unconscious, and they were wary of being tracked. As soon as they got back to the city in the wee hours of the morning, they found themselves a lodge and slept.

When the sun was out and the shops open, they checked out and bought burner phones.

"Why do we need new phones?" Chanel asked.

Adonis smiled. "Burner phones. You need to call your mum and so do I. This is the safest way to avoid being tracked. So, all communication should be through these," Adonis said, handing it to her.

Adonis then walked with her the breadth of the city, until

they got to a part of town neither of them often went. There they took a taxi towards the Bonsai beachfront ten miles away, a place familiar to Adonis. They used to go clubbing there with Dmitri and sometimes stayed at a friend's place. This house was usually empty for about six months a year because their friend would travel a lot. Nevertheless, since he didn't want to sell the place, he would allow either Dmitri or Adonis stay there, especially if there was an emergency. Two days ago, Adonis had given him a call and asked if the place was still available. When he got the green light, he only waited for the right moment to make their move.

They were there after a forty-minute ride. Tucked away in one of the narrow streets, it was a townhouse that overlooked the ocean below. An old design, it was not huge, as in the past such houses were crammed into a narrow stretch of beachfront. But its three bedrooms and other amenities were more than enough for the two of them. They were able to get a good view of anyone accessing the street from the front door, and it had a stunning view of the ocean beyond. It also had an advantage that Adonis loved – a secret passageway that led to the beach below. If they were tracked down, they still had a chance to escape.

Chanel loved the place immediately. It had the old school architecture that she had studied in high school. It was the kind of place she would one day own when the millions came in.

After freshening up, they both went to stand on the balcony overlooking the open ocean. The breeze that hit them ruffled their clothes and hair and had them giggling like kids who had hit the jackpot. They had done it. They were no longer in the clutches of Gunner and Vernon. They could start afresh.

Swept up by the euphoria of the moment, they were drawn to each other. Chanel led Adonis by the hand back into the bedroom, placing herself on the bed. He lowered himself gently to her and they soon felt into a slow session of kissing. He disrobed her gently, and when the sun revealed her beautiful body to him, he knew he was in love. She received him and they were soon in a tight embrace of deep sighs and moans of pleasure. That place made you forget time. They felt they could go on for hours, and so they did.

It was only after the sun had set over the horizon that they both realized there was nothing to eat in the house. That was nothing to worry about, because it gave them the chance to walk the charmed narrow streets like two newlyweds on their honeymoon. Every other care in the world was forgotten.

When the tour bus driver found Gunner, he took him to the nearest emergency hospital. Gunner came to three hours after he arrived in the ward and was quick to ask to be discharged.

He took another couple of hours before he could get a full grasp of what had happened. Adonis had taken away his artist. They both knew something about the rootkit, and AI system, so that wasn't good for business. They needed to be reined in, there was too much at stake. When he told his boss about it all, his henchmen had already started tracking the escapees.

After forty-eight hours searching, Gunner received the report that they were nowhere to be found. They had covered their tracks better than expected. He had been set up, so he needed to change his approach and draw them out of hiding. He didn't want to make the call to the clean-up crew, because it often meant there was going to be death involved. It was simply what they were trained to do, even when it wasn't necessary.

However, he had no other option.

↑

While Adonis went about prepping the sausages for breakfast one morning, Chanel went into the bathroom. She switched on her phone and received a flurry of texts. Those she really wanted to read were from her mother. She decided to call her.

"Baby, how are you?" her mother asked, relief in her voice.

"I'm okay, Mom. How are things at home?"

"They are fine, darling. How is the tour? Are you done yet?" her mother asked.

Chanel paused briefly then replied, "Yes, it's going okay. Very well actually. Still on the road."

"Where are you?" her mother asked.

"Still on the road. I'm not sure where because I've never been here before," Chanel replied.

"That's fine, baby. Is there any landmark close by that can give you an idea of where you are?"

It was at that moment that Chanel sensed there was someone else on the line. She couldn't explain how. She just knew. She kept quiet for a moment, listening. She could hear whispering in the background, as if someone was instructing her mother on what to say.

"Chanel?"

"I love you, Mum. Bye," Chanel quickly said, and hung

up. She took in a deep breath. In all her calls home, her mother had never asked for a landmark. She never cared about such specifics. She hoped she was wrong, but something wasn't right. She flushed the toilet and headed to the kitchen.

Adonis was working on another batch of sausages.

"You sure you're doing it right?" she teased.

"In my home, Ma insisted we had to know how to cook for ourselves. That wasn't negotiable!" Adonis replied with a smile.

Suddenly, Chanel's phone rang. Adonis froze, looking at her.

"Why is your phone on?" he asked sternly.

"I was just checking a message, that's all," she replied.

She took it out and looked at the screen. It was her mother.

"It's Mum. I'm not sure I should pick it," Chanel said nervously.

He nodded and she took the call. The voice was familiar, but it wasn't her mother.

"Hello, Chanel. I'm sure you know who's speaking. I was disappointed that your fine bottle of vodka was not so good after all. At least for me. We wasted a celebration. I hope we can make up for that by allowing me to host a proper party now that the album tour ended a little prematurely. It will be good for you to come back to the office and talk about things. I have a few great ideas that I shared with both your parents here and they like them. They are looking forward to seeing you soon. Don't keep them waiting."

The line went dead, leaving Chanel shell-shocked.

Adonis noticed her expression. "What's wrong?"

Chanel dropped the phone and put her hands to her head.

"Who was that? Talk to me!" Adonis demanded.

"That was Gunner. He wants us to go back," she mumbled.

"Too bad for him! He can go hang himself!" Adonis exclaimed.

"He says he's got both our parents with him."

Adonis' face scowled with anger.

"Dammit!" he shouted, throwing the spatula he was holding across the room.

"We need to call the cops," Chanel said.

"No, we can't call the cops," he replied.

"Why not?"

"Because They won't save us! Do you think all these artists died without the cops knowing who did it?"

"What do we do then?" a teary Chanel asked.

"I don't know! I don't know!" Adonis shouted in frustration. He knew the tables had turned and his mind couldn't think.

Lost in his thoughts, smoke started filling the kitchen as the sausages burned to a crisp.

"We're going to burn the house down!" Chanel shouted.

Adonis spun round and saw smoke billowing to the ceiling, with small flames rising off the pan. He quickly switched off the cooker.

He looked around the kitchen – there was no fire extinguisher in sight. He dashed to the living room and grabbed a large shawl. He drenched it in water and threw it over the pan.

The fire died, and all that was left was a charred pan, a hazy cloud of smoke and a choking smell. They opened all the windows they could to ease the intensity.

With the disaster averted, they both realized they still had the first batch of sausages, but their appetites were gone.

"We need to go to the cops," Chanel suggested again.

"Like I told you before, that won't work. We could end up losing our folks and the police will cover it up. I can guarantee that," Adonis replied.

"So, what do we do?"

"We have to meet him."

Chanel's eyes widened.

"Meet who, Gunner?" she asked.

"Yeah."

"For what?"

"Do you want him to hold on to your parents when we are the ones he really wants? Our parents have nothing to do with this. We have to exchange our freedom for theirs," Adonis replied.

Chanel shook her head as she pondered this.

"Do you trust him?" she asked.

"I have never trusted Gunner. But we don't have a choice in this," Adonis said with resignation.

"What if he screws us over?"

Adonis sighed. "If he screws us then it is what it is. We are screwed," he replied.

They sat in silence for a few more moments.

"So, I guess we have to call him then?" Chanel asked.

"Yeah."

She handed him the burner phone, but he scoffed at it.

"No point in hiding now," Adonis said.

She gave him her phone. Adonis dialed Gunner's number and waited.

"Have you come to a decision?" Gunner's voice crackled over the phone.

"Yeah…. We were thinking we can do an exchange," Adonis said.

"I'm listening," Gunner replied.

"Chanel and I will come together to a place we agree to. Just the two of us. You will come with our parents. Just you and our parents. You will let them go and we will hand ourselves over to you. That's our offer," Adonis said as confidently as he could muster.

Gunner gave a long, grating laugh.

"I can see you've given this some thought. Fair enough. Where do we do this?" he asked.

"At Mathews Point. It's a lookout spot facing the ocean," Adonis suggested.

"That's quite a drive away," Gunner remarked.

"We are both making some sacrifices."

Gunner paused.

"All right. It's a deal. This evening at seven," Gunner replied.

"Let's do it earlier," Adonis proposed.

"Don't test me, A.D."

"I wouldn't do that. There's too much to lose," Adonis said.

"Indeed. Daylight won't do it for me, so the time remains the same. Seven it is."

Adonis hated it, but caved in.

"See you then."

He hung up and turned to Chanel. "We're on."

†

While standing at the balcony watching the ocean waves slap onto the shore, Adonis and Chanel discussed how they would do the exchange.

"Are we doing this the same way they do it in the movies?" Chanel asked.

"It can't be. They have guns, we don't," Adonis replied.

"We can get one—"

"With what cash? I'm nearly maxed out."

"So, we'll just stand there and hope for the best?" Chanel posed.

"He can't hurt us. We know too much," Adonis tried to reassure her.

"That is actually a good reason for him to hurt us. To silence us," Chanel said.

"But hurting you can make things go bad for them," Adonis asserted.

"How? No one knows what we know," Chanel replied, "The police don't know, no reporter knows. We'll just die. We have no leverage!"

Chanel's words jarred Adonis. She had a good point. He suddenly clapped his hands once, as if a lightbulb went on in his head.

"I've got it!" Adonis exclaimed.

"What?" Chanel asked.

"Wait here," he said.

Adonis walked back into the apartment, heading towards the bedroom. Moments later, he came back with his phone.

"What do you want to do?" a curious Chanel asked.

"We're going to record our story. From start to finish," Adonis said with excitement.

"On the phone?" Chanel asked quizzically.

"It's all we have left. That's our leverage."

"How is it going to be our leverage? It will still be in our phones and nothing will happen!"

"Trust me, I'll get it out there. No matter what. With this, they won't take things too far because they won't want the world to know their murderous history," Adonis replied.

"Blackmail is what I'm hearing."

"You got that right! It's an ace up our sleeve if they try to screw us. Ready?"

Chanel nodded. "Ready."

🌴

Dmitri had been getting more comfortable with each passing day.

It was probably an effect of hanging around Kai. His biker brother simply oozed testosterone and was often doing something. Dmitri admired this zest for life and wanted to do better than just being a couch potato hiding in fear. To break the monotony of indoor living, Dmitri would put on a helmet and ride along with Kai to the shopping center or to a biker meet. No one could tell who he was when he wore a helmet, so he had more confidence moving about.

This growth in confidence made him start switching on his phone for short periods. He started doing this at night first, when he felt people were asleep and no one would call him. He then started doing five minutes here and there during the day, mostly just before he left a location that was not home.

Today, they were riding to another biker meet. However, they stopped over at the garage to have the bike's radiator checked. An hour later, the job was done. Knowing they would be leaving soon, Dmitri switched on his phone to check for messages. As usual, he found several voice mails from Adonis. They didn't say much, just that he would like to talk.

Normally Adonis would give details of what he was calling for, but the latest voicemails were pretty short and guarded, as if he was being cautious about what he said. This made Dmitri suspicious, because it was unlike his friend. That's why he had never replied or called back. He didn't know what was going on with Adonis. He could be working for the enemy.

He was just about switch it off when his phone rang. Adonis's name popped on the screen and Dmitri hesitated. After staring at it for a few seconds, curiosity took over and he answered the call.

"Dammit man! What's wrong with you?" Adonis exclaimed, surprised that the call went through.

"Hey A.D. What's good?" Dmitri replied.

"What's good? You're asking me what's good? Hearing your voice is what's good!" Adonis said.

"Good to hear yours too," Dmitri replied, his ears on overdrive trying to listen and detect anything unusual.

"I hope you are good. Listen. I can't talk much because maybe I'm being tracked. I need a favor."

Dmitri's alarmist thoughts grew stronger, but he couldn't hang up on his best friend.

"What's going on A.D?" Dmitri asked.

"Look. I ran off with Chanel."

"You what?" Dmitri said.

"Not eloping or anything. I just needed to get away from the company," Adonis replied.

"So, what's going on now?" Dmitri asked.

"They took our parents hostage," Adonis replied.

"Fucking Hell! When?"

"I don't know when. That's why I need your help."

"What do you want me to do? Call the cops? I have no cash for ransom you know," Dmitri remarked.

"I'm not asking you for ransom! Chanel and I are the ransom."

"Hold on. What do you mean by that?" Dmitri asked.

"I've just sent you an email. In case something happens to me, send it to the cops and to the newspapers," Adonis said, ignoring his friend's question.

"How will I know something's happened to you?"

"If you haven't heard from me by eight tonight, come to Mathews Point and find me," Adonis said.

"It's near the party house, right?" Dmitri asked.

"You know it! So, can I count on you?"

Dmitri sighed. "I've got your back," he assured Adonis.

"Thanks! Gotta go. And Dmitri?"

"Yeah?"

"You've been a good brother to me. Thank you."

Then the line went dead.

"Aye! Let's get out of here!" Kai shouted at Dmitri as the bike came to life with a loud roar.

As Dmitri put on his helmet, he couldn't shake off the feeling that he had just said his last goodbye to his best friend.

✳

Adonis and Chanel rode in silence in the back of a taxi, her hand tightly clutching his as they gazed at the streets outside.

When they arrived at the Mathew Fort lookout point, there was no other vehicle there. The curry shops and small cafeteria were also closed. It wasn't an iconic spot, but it was well known. The light was beginning to fade even out to the ocean, and you could barely see the ocean water catching the occasional shimmer off the waves. The lookout point was well known for two things: watching a beautiful sunrise off the horizon and the view of ships coming into the harbor on the other side of the island. The lookout point had no big hotels or residences in the area, so it was rare to find any visitors at the spot after six in the evening, especially on a weekday.

Adonis scanned the place, looking around for anything unusual. Although he spotted nothing, this made him more nervous. He didn't like surprises, and he had no back up whatsoever other than the call he made to Dmitri. So, they waited.

It was forty minutes later, when the streets were dark, that two cars rolled into the parking area.

Adonis braced himself.

Gunner got out of the car with his henchmen in tow. "You two have had me worried," he said.

Adonis doubted it. Gunner rarely worried. He was a practical man who believed in cause and effect. Adonis was more concerned that Gunner had his henchmen with him.

"Why did you do it?" Gunner asked.

"I needed some space to think," Chanel said.

"In the middle of a tour?" Gunner posed.

"Did somebody die?" Chanel snapped.

Adonis winced at her. She was trying to rile up Gunner, and this wasn't a good idea.

"She just needed to get her head together," Adonis chimed in.

"I'm not sure that worked, judging by how she's talking to me," Gunner said.

Adonis nudged Chanel.

"I'm sorry," she said, picking up the cue.

"No offense taken," Gunner replied.

"Where are our parents?" Adonis asked.

"They are waiting for you. You didn't expect me to bring them here at their age?"

Adonis gulped. This wasn't part of the agreement. He exchanged a look with Chanel.

"Where are they?" Adonis asked.

"At the office – a place where we can all talk as a family. There's no need for this exchange thing. We still want to work together," Gunner said.

Adonis and Chanel looked at each other again. Adonis nodded at her.

"What's the catch?" Chanel asked.

"We have a dream we are building here. I simply need you to promise me it won't happen again," Gunner said.

"It won't," Chanel replied.

Gunner smiled. "Good stuff! All right, let's go meet them."

One of Gunner's men opened the rear door to the first car. Chanel and Adonis walked towards it. Chanel got in first and as Adonis was about to follow her, the henchman held him back.

"What?" Adonis asked.

"You will travel separately," Gunner said, "You both deserve to be treated better. A car each to yourselves is a show of my commitment to this."

Adonis reluctantly walked to the second car and got into the back seat. He was sandwiched between two hefty men.

The trip began, Adonis judging it would be at least an hour to the Sephtis office.

They were fifteen minutes into the trip when suddenly the

car carrying Adonis took a sharp right turn, leaving the other car to keep going on its own.

"Hey, what—" Adonis started, but he didn't finish his sentence.

One man threw a black hood over Adonis's head as the other grabbed his arms. As Adonis wrestled, his hands were tied together using plastic cable ties, followed by his legs. In less than a minute he was unable to move and didn't know where he was being taken.

🌴

Adonis could hear the incessant banging of a metal window high above him, but he couldn't see it. He was still covered by the hood, tied to a chair. He had been there for what seemed like an hour, and no one had spoken to him. He figured Chanel had already arrived at Sephtis, or even worse, been tied up just like him. It was chilly inside, and he shivered slightly every few minutes.

Adonis heard footsteps walking toward him. The hood came off, and he could finally breathe better. He inhaled deeply, but the air that filled his nostrils was rich with the scent of gasoline. He looked around him. He was in an abandoned warehouse, possibly one used for delivery trucks. Empty wooden crates were stacked in different parts of the large open space. There were some fluorescent lights dotting the ceiling, but most were not working.

His eyes lowered, and he noted that two henchmen were lurking in the shadows, watching him. His eyes settled on a table in front of him. Seated there was Gunner, who had a

Genesys tablet in front of him. Gunner's eyes stared intensely at Adonis. Adonis felt his fear rising.

"Where's Chanel?" Adonis asked.

"I believed in you," Gunner said.

"Where's Chanel? What have you done with her?"

Gunner turned the tablet over so that it faced Adonis.

On the screen was a live video feed of Terek.

"He's been waiting for you for a long time," Gunner said.

"What is this? What are you showing me?"

"Who have you been speaking to, Adonis?"

"What are you talking about?"

"Whom have you told what you know?" Gunner persisted.

"No one!"

"Take him out," Gunner ordered.

On screen, Adonis saw Terek's head lifted up by a man's hand. Terek's bloodied face stared into the camera filming him, as if asking for help.

"What are you doing?" Adonis whispered in dread.

A gun barrel was placed to the side of Terek's head and a hand pulled the trigger. The bullet's impact made Terek's head wobble as it went through his head. He collapsed in the seat, never to rise again.

Adonis's face was filled with horror. His numbing fear was more for his mother than the father whose death he had just witnessed.

"Where's my Ma? Where is she!" he shouted, struggling to wriggle free of the seat.

"Listen carefully. If you don't tell me what I want to know, that's not the first video of someone dying you will watch. Chanel and her parents are waiting in line. This is make or break for you. So, tell me, what is it going to be?" Gunner posed menacingly.

Confused, Adonis's mind went blank.

CHAPTER SEVENTEEN

KAI'S BIKER GANG meets were always outdoors and something to behold. On a small island like Tropicon, they really stood out with their leather jackets, scruffy jeans, leather boots, and tattooed necks. Most of them were between their late twenties and early forties. In the past, they would allow a can of alcohol each during meets, but this was banned after one of them crashed in a freak accident. Nowadays they walked around with sodas and tonic waters as they had lively conversations. Another big change was the recent uptake of high-performance electric bikes, which had overcome initial skepticism by purists. The meet was at an abandoned parking lot near the beach, and there was plenty of grilled meat and music as usual. Sometimes the meets would run late into the night. It was always good fun.

This one was not enjoyable for Dmitri. He had waited for

Adonis to call after it got to eight in the evening. Ten minutes later, he figured that his friend might be in trouble and he switched to plan B. He walked to where Kai was talking to a fellow biker.

"Kai, it's happening," Dmitri said.

Kai, jovial at first, quickly changed and moved aside with Dmitri.

"He hasn't called?" Kai asked.

"No. I tried calling, and he's not responding. His phone might be on silent because I can still see its location."

"Where is he?"

"Around ten miles from Mathews Point."

"Keep tracking it," his brother instructed.

Kai then walked over to the group and called them to attention.

"I need ten of you for a favor. It's a night-out-on-the-town kind of thing," Kai bellowed.

"Run and gun?" someone asked.

"Run and gun," Kai replied.

"What if more of us want to join in? We can't just let you guys go out there alone. It's been a while," another biker said.

"I'm not holding you back. So long as you are under my command," Kai said.

Minutes later, the engines roared to life, and that's how a convoy of twenty motorcycles ended up rolling down the highway towards the beachfront.

↑

"This is not a game, son!" Gunner shouted.

As soon as he said this, he landed another punch on

Adonis's face, knocking him over. Adonis landed on his side with a thud. He was still tied to the chair, so he couldn't pick himself up.

Adonis groaned. He had stopped counting the number of blows he had received. All he could taste was blood in his mouth. His right eye was swelling first, but he could still see through it.

"The more you waste my time, the more dangerous it becomes for them. And here I was thinking you cared about others more than you cared about yourself!" Gunner said, as he landed kicks to Adonis's ribs.

As he was being hit, Adonis tried not to dwell on the pain. He blocked it out with a memory from his childhood. He remembered himself playing on a swing on a sunny afternoon. All he could hear was the chirping of birds and the wind blowing into the trees. He had learned to do it when he was younger when he started having nightmares. They had started after his father Terek got used to beating up his mother. Her screams would fill his dreams to the point he couldn't sleep. They persisted even after Terek left, and his mother shared with him the technique she was using to heal.

Sun. Swing. Birds. Repeat.

He didn't want to mention the recording yet, though he was tempted. The idea was to drive Gunner to his breaking point, when he would realize he was getting nowhere with the beatings. Then, and only then, would it be effective. Adonis prayed his body would hang on for longer.

"Leave him to me!" a voice said.

The kicks had stopped. Adonis, whose eyes were closed, spat out some blood then slowly opened his eyes. His vision skewed due to the fact he was lying on his side, he barely made out the tall, hulking form of Vernon.

Vernon took off the coat his was wearing and walked up to Adonis. With his left arm, he grabbed Adonis and lifted him up off the ground. Adonis steadied himself as he sat up again. The pain came back again, and his ribs were on fire.

"How are we doing today, Adonis?" Vernon asked in a courteous voice.

"Yesterday… was a little… better," Adonis managed to mumble.

"I can see that. What do you think we should do about it?" Vernon asked, sitting himself on the table.

Adonis coughed out some more blood.

"We should…end it?" he whispered.

"What does ending it mean?"

"Just… stop. Let my parents go."

Vernon folded the sleeves of his shirt to elbow length.

"I want to do that. But you stole something that belongs to me."

"Chanel is not property. She's a person," Adonis said.

Vernon laughed.

"Touché. I'll rephrase, for your sake. She's a person that belongs to me. My tech belongs to me. The data on that tech all belongs to me, and you stole various elements of it. Why? Who are you working for?" Vernon asked.

"I'm working for nobody."

"Then why do it?"

"I could ask you the same question. Why kill your artists?"

Vernon paused and stared at Adonis for what seemed like a long time.

"Do you believe I killed someone?" Vernon asked.

"I know you killed someone. Oceania," Adonis replied.

"That's a very dangerous assertion."

"You are a very dangerous man."

Vernon licked his lips. Deciding he didn't need it, he unbuttoned his shirt and took it off, revealing a muscular torso in a white vest.

"Is there anyone else who knows about your wild allegations?"

Adonis thought about the response he needed to give. Then he realized he had nothing more to give.

"If something happens to me, the whole world will know."

"Say what?" Gunner asked, unsure he heard him right.

"Repeat what you said for Gunner's sake," Vernon told Adonis.

Adonis cleared his throat.

"If anything happens to me, then the whole world will know," he said.

Vernon motioned for the tablet. It was brought to him. He swiped the screen a few times, and then held up the screen for Adonis.

Adonis saw Chanel and her parents in the frame. Their mouths were taped up so they couldn't speak. He could see the fear and desperation in their eyes.

"Does that threat include them too?" Vernon asked.

"Yes, it does," Adonis quickly said. He needed to save them if he could. He just wished he knew where they were being held.

"How sure can I be?" Vernon asked.

"You just have to trust me," Adonis replied.

"But I don't trust you. You have so far refused to give us any information. I need to know that you're not lying."

"I'm not lying to you!"

"There's only one way to find out," Vernon said.

Adonis knew what this meant, and he had no way to stop it.

↑

The biker gang stopped short of the turnoff that led to the location Dmitri's tracker had pinpointed. Moving in such a large group with loud engines was going to attract attention. Some bikers used the more silent electric bikes to get closer while the rest walked in. In the near distance were two warehouses along the beachfront. One of them was their destination.

Kai and another biker, who both had military experience, split the group into two. One team would scope the first warehouse and the rest would handle the second one. Whoever found Adonis would alert the rest and they would go and back up the other team. To Dmitri's amazement, everyone was armed: from regular handguns, to rifles, and two shotguns. This was a proper cavalry.

Each team had a scout who went to check scope the two warehouses, and it didn't take them long to figure out where Adonis was being held. Two henchmen stood guard outside a small side door to the second warehouse. Three SUVs were also parked outside.

With this determined, they made their move. Two men took out the guards outside with strangleholds. They managed to open the door. As fifteen went in, five bikers remained outside as lookouts.

They determined that Adonis was being held in a room divided by a partition. It was as they headed there that they bumped into one of the henchmen, who saw men clad in leather that he didn't recognize. He made the mistake of firing his handgun. As soon as the bikers cut him down, all hell broke loose.

↑

When the first gunshots rang out, Vernon froze. Gunner and one henchman moved towards the partition door. Two other henchmen in the room positioned themselves, guns at the ready.

"Who's there?" Gunner shouted.

His answer came in gunshots. Many gunshots.

As Gunner and Vernon threw themselves to the floor, the henchmen returned fire. They were hit, one after the other. Adonis was already low, but he threw himself to the floor when a bullet whizzed past his ear.

The bullets stopped, and it was quiet for a moment. Adonis heard Vernon move behind some crates.

Gunner was slinking away from the partition door when it came open. He fired and hit one of the bikers in the leg. He fell, but he fired back at the same time, catching Gunner on his shoulder, causing him to drop his gun as he grimaced in pain.

Kai walked in with a shotgun in hand. When Gunner saw this, he tried reaching for his gun again. Kai wasn't going to let that happen, pumping two rounds into Gunner. Gunner collapsed in a bloody heap, dead.

"Are you okay?" Kai asked as he rushed to Adonis.

"Yeah… yes, I am," Adonis replied.

"Sorry we had to come in hot," Kai said, as he cut the rope cords.

Adonis leaned forward. "There's one more behind the crates," he whispered.

His cords cut, Kai told Adonis to stay down as a precaution. Kai cocked his shotgun.

"I know you're somewhere behind those crates. I suggest you come out without using your gun!" Kai ordered.

Nothing happened.

"I'll say it one more time. If you want to stay alive get out without using your gun!" Kai bellowed.

Nothing.

He fired two rounds into some crates, splintering them into pieces.

"All right! I'm coming out!" Vernon shouted.

He walked out from the behind the crates, hands in the air.

Kai trained his gun on him until one of the bikers tied Vernon's hands behind his back. They sat him in the chair Adonis had sat on.

As Vernon sat there, he didn't look scared. He locked eyes with Adonis as sirens rang from a distance.

"I wouldn't want to be here when they arrive," Vernon said with a smile.

Adonis wasn't amused.

Mustering the little energy, he had left, he flew in with a kick that landed square on Vernon's chest, toppling him over. He hit the floor with a resounding thud.

"Piece of shit! This is not going to play out the way you think it will," Adonis snapped.

↑

After taking Vernon into custody, Adonis and Dmitri went with the police to track down Chanel using her phone. She wasn't far from where he had been held. Half an hour was all it took as the tracker led them to an old car repair shop that was closed.

Having surrounded it, the police used a battering ram to gain entry from the front and the rear, trying to catch them by surprise. Dmitri and Adonis watched as two of Gunner's henchmen came out with their hands in the air. They didn't put up a fight.

"Chanel!" Adonis shouted as he ran towards the shop. A policeman stopped him in his tracks.

"Let me in!" Adonis said.

"Officers only, son," the cop replied.

After a few minutes, the police had not yet emerged, and Adonis wasn't happy about that. Without warning, he made a dash for it.

"Hey! Stop!" the cop shouted. Adonis didn't slow down.

When he got in, he discovered the reason why the woman he loved hadn't responded to his call. Lying on the dusty concrete floor near a broken-down sedan was Chanel. Her eyes were closed, and her face was covered in grime. She was dead, blood flowing from a bullet wound in her chest. Next to her lay her two parents, who were in each other's arms even in death.

Adonis fell to his knees as tears flowed freely down his cheeks.

He had failed her.

↑

The next few days were difficult.

Adonis spent two days in the hospital being treated for

his injuries, but he struggled to sleep. The police came twice during his hospital stay to record a statement. When he was discharged, he learned that they had raided the Sephtis offices and arrested the staff. Natasha was still at the office when she was arrested, thinking that Vernon's operation was still in play. After years running from the authorities, her time had run out too.

Leroy was also arrested, but Adonis said a word for him, and he wasn't detained for long. The police seized all the equipment in FXX AI and had their computer forensics team poring over the algorithms, which were still intact.

Soon after that the whole office was shut down.

Adonis joined his mother and sisters at his father's funeral. A few of Terek's former bandmates travelled to see them when they heard the news. Most of the mourners were people who knew his mother and her children. Terek didn't leave many people in the world with fond memories of him, Adonis concluded. His mother and sisters were broken, and he resolved to support them in their grief. He would need his own time to process what his father meant to him.

Adonis then spent a few days sleeping his trauma away before attending Chanel's funeral. Her aunt, who had even visited him at hospital, had organized it.

"I tried to save her," he told the aunt, and then broke down. She held hugged him close that day, like he was family.

Adonis had thought of not attending her funeral, and then changed his mind. Not surprisingly, it was more painful losing her than it was losing his father Terek.

The funeral was long, and afterwards Adonis spent time with the extended family, telling them about Chanel's talent and her aspirations. It helped him heal somewhat, for he was not mourning alone.

The next couple of weeks had Adonis feeling safer than he had in many weeks. This endured until Vernon's court case. Adonis and Dmitri testified against him and gave the court as much information as they could.

Due to his crack team of lawyers, Vernon put up a strong case. However, no one was prepared for the verdict. Vernon was sentenced to just four years in prison and would be eligible for parole in just two years. This news rattled the island residents who had followed the case closely. It also angered them because it was a sign of the corrupt system that always seemed to favor the rich in every sphere of life. Justice was rare to find on Tropicon Islands if the accused had deep pockets.

This was one of several things making Adonis restless as he lay on a pool chair at the beach bar. Next to him was Dmitri, also lying on a pool chair soaking in the warm afternoon sun. Caribbean music played in the background. Women with bikinis and men with trunk shorts walked up and down the shoreline, occasionally breaking the two men's view of the ocean water before them.

"Remember that time you wanted to be a surfer?" Dmitri asked.

"We both wanted to be surfers," Adonis replied with a smile.

"Yeah, but you wanted it more."

"I wanted it more because I was drunk on whiskey at the time, and I wanted to convince a girl that I was an adrenaline junkie," Adonis clarified.

"But you are an adrenaline junkie," Dmitri said. "Do you realize that even?"

"How?"

"You've pushed the envelope the last few months—"

"Stop it. Just... don't," Adonis warned his friend.

Dmitri realized he had triggered something. "Sorry, I didn't mean it that way."

Adonis knew where Dmitri was going. He didn't need it, because it always led to him to question whether Chanel would still be alive if he had held back. This was his greatest burden.

"Look, I still have the dream to get our business up and running. We both know it has the potential to change how the world experiences music," Dmitri said.

"Yeah, but how fast can we do it?" Adonis asked.

"You have to take your time to do it right," Dmitri replied.

Adonis sighed. "It won't be fast enough to make people forget Sephtis."

"This is a capitalist world for the most part. Trust me, they will forget," Dmitri replied.

"Will it be up and running before Vernon gets out?" Adonis asked unconvinced.

"It doesn't matter. What will Vernon do? He will never be in the business again," Dmitri posed.

"Systems like his don't just collapse overnight."

"He's behind bars, A.D. The prosecutor is appealing the light sentence too," Dmitri said.

"It won't be enough. Can't you see that? He killed Chanel and my unborn child," Adonis retorted.

There was a tense silence between them.

"What are you going to do about it?" Dmitri asked.

Adonis's mind was already full of things he wanted to do. He just wanted to settle on one that would ease the restlessness in his soul.

"Are you afraid that his sentence will still be a short one?" Dmitri prodded further.

"Not really. I think that's a good thing," Adonis replied.

"Why?" Dmitri asked, slightly surprised.

"Because I'll be prepared for him when he comes out," Adonis said calmly.